Network
Sleeper

Richard M Marshall

This book was originally written in 1998, extended in 1999 following publisher feedback and then finally revised for Amazon publication in 2014 after initial reworking in 2010 for self publishing on another system.

Thanks to all who provided feedback on the early drafts, especially my Mother who is a great writer herself.

ISBN-13: 978-1497386310

one

The alarm went off as usual at 7.28, to catch a couple of minutes of music and then the news at half past. Although Ian had more news flowing into his house than most newspaper offices he still liked listening to the items chosen for inclusion in CultureNet's sound channel news coverage. That way he knew the network was working.

For the last ten years it had been more or less the same: European and North American politics, news from the performing arts and then some brief news about finance. With CultureNet's eclectic mix of late twentieth century music it appealed to impoverished performers and comparatively wealthy intellectuals. Or that is what Ian liked to think.

Normally he would lie for a few minutes listening to some piece of music before going to the bathroom. But this morning something was wrong. There was a news piece that said that a fascist candidate for the Southern Italian regional parliament had won a landslide victory. But following that there were no associated changes in the Bourse. The European stock market always dipped when an extremist was elected, some kind of instinctive reaction. But that item was missing.

Ian leapt out of bed, pulling on a T-shirt and running tights and ran through to the office in his combined abode and workplace. The office was a huge, darkened space containing many machines, some of them very old. As he entered the room a few dim lights came on and a few images appeared on the work wall. They showed the mail that had come in during the night, but that was not what he wanted to look at first. He went to his desk, and pointed at an item on its matt surface. The mail screen faded into a list of news items, headlines readable but the text small. He looked for the item about the elections in Southern Italy. There it was, complete with the name of the journalist who had submitted it, as well as its authentication record. As he looked at it the detail text zoomed into readability and he could see the record of its short journey through the system.

Next Ian checked out the reports from the Bourse. Nothing relating to Southern Italian stocks at all. That was wrong. Next he asked for the news ship list, the information being sent to radio and television stations around the world for broadcast. The item was gone. That was very wrong, an item like that should stay there for at least six hours before retiring itself. He checked the news item and saw that it had a life of only five minutes.

Just as he settled into his high-backed chair to think about what could have happened, the phone rang.

———————

Some things do not change. There are always the repressed and the tortured, those deprived of their right to freedom. For one hundred years these people have risked their lives to learn the truth about world events, information that their rulers regarded as too dangerous for them to learn. Information is power. The world's oppressed had come to rely on the BBC World Service for unbiased, reliable information round the world. Although the name BBC was a double anachronism, it was still the world's most reliable source of news.

Last century the BBC had been a kind of public service, paid from a tax on television owners. Then it had been sold off. Soon the BBC was broken into many parts. The broadcasting service was sold to commercial operators; the drama and entertainment wing was bought by Sony and continued as it always had, creating the best television dramas in the world.

That left a worldwide news gathering network and the World Service. The World Service was not a commercial proposition, so there was wide fear that it would close, but a grant from the Sainsbury Foundation to Amnesty International ensured that there was a continuing feed of unbiased news to the needy around the world.

That left the journalists, all of them at the top of their profession and many of them household names, and a complete machine for taking the information they gathered and channelling it into broadcasting. Reuters had seen that, and bought the lot to form WIN, the World Information Network. Information is valuable, and its reliable, rapid delivery a service for which people will pay a premium price.

WIN sells news to whoever will pay for it. Newspapers and broadcasters buy it. They browse the ship list for interesting items, and pick out what they consider suitable for their readers and viewers. For music stations WIN provides an automated service that generates local-language news bulletins for inclusion in their programming. Other news deliverers, such as CNN, surf the full news source, seeking out interesting items, searching deeper, as they add their own value to the news feed.

But other customers buy raw news too. Big companies, institutions, even governments, buy information about what is happening to the world. Absorbing it all and drawing their own private conclusions. At first the information had been fed through analysts who gave advice or made decisions. Traders buying and selling mysterious commodities would listen to the information and act accordingly. But over the years much of this was automated. With a completely reliable source of information, computers had taken over the mundane process of making buy and sell decisions across the world's markets.

Completely reliable until this morning.

Ian let the phone ring for a while before answering. Up on the work wall it showed that the call was from Xavier Mann, described as being a Permanent Network consultant. Ian pressed an area on the desk, not holding with voice control, and Xavier's face appeared on the wall.

"We've been hacked," he said.

"I know," replied Ian. "I heard the news item about the Italian election that was only shipped for a few minutes."

"I'm pleased to hear you're as sharp as your reputation holds. The question is how did it happen. Can you manage a meeting now?"

Ian suddenly realised that he had been lost in the world of news and information and had not listened to his body. Currently it was calling for the bathroom and an espresso. "No," he replied. "Half an hour."

"Cool, I'll get the others together for 9 then. Give you a chance to get ready." chirped Xavier, and the image disappeared, leaving Ian to wander through to his living area.

———————

Back at the turn of the century people commuted long distances from where they lived to where they worked. People who lived in the centres of the cities worked outside, and most people lived out of town and travelled long, pointless hours into the centre.

In 2013 the Change started. Pollution, fuel shortages and a century's cumulative fatigue led to increasing discontent amongst the educated. Why spend three hours of a day doing nothing useful. Employers started to think the same. Workers arrived late, tired and irritable and left early to beat the rush. Of course they never could, losing yet more of their lives, their families, and their health.

Computer people had been the first to revolt, as being the best adapted to village working. They understood networks and teleworking. They understood how meetings and office noise made you lose concentration and time. Then everyone followed. Instead of sprawling dormitories, suburbs and office parks, employment started to return to where the employees were. The Villages started forming, each a complete community of work and living.

The Change left many large office blocks empty; whole floors of quality buildings abandoned in a mess of partitions and clutter. Some people, seeking peace, space and independence started to move into the offices and convert them into combined living and work spaces. Original architecture and design were key, using recovered materials and contemporary art.

Ian's apartment was like that, formed from a complete floor of a huge office block outside Edinburgh, Scotland. Although there was virtually no local work for someone of his talents, he liked living there, with its many festivals, and near his family. He did his best work there, in his darkened workspace, listening to strange music, sealed away from the world. Of course he might be working remotely, on the other side of the planet; it did not really matter. His network connections saw to that.

Emerging from the workspace he wandered over to the bathroom. One of the missing features of offices, the early settlers had found, were bathrooms. So they applied all their creativity to building interesting and comfortable spaces for the mundane task of washing. In any case, there was no shortage of space. Ian's bathroom was surrounded by a rainbow of plastic sheeting, arranged spirally to form a private central room.

The shower cubicle had many heads at different angles, surrounded by massive slabs of glass that had once formed some pompous manager's office. The bath was a work of art, created for him by a French company called Plomb'Art. It was made of multi-coloured resin with hundreds of water jets set into it and tumbling around it down to the ground.

The washbasins were from an old hotel lavatory. Two scoops cut out of marble-like material, now suspended on old scaffolding bars. He reflected sadly on how the other basin was not too useful just right now. Funny how he always used the same one, the other one reserved for some girlfriend who somehow never seemed to stay around long enough for using it to become a habit.

He went through to the kitchen and pulled the curtains open to reveal a view over a half disused road and on to trees. The security screens had already opened. The kitchen table had once been used for meetings; the storage cupboards had once held paper files. The cooker was massive and powered from a large bottle of gas sitting beside it. Plomb'Art had been at work here too, shaping a vent over the cooker from old air conditioning ducts reshaped into a fish head. The sink was formed from a slab of hard metal, hammered to form a series of water pools.

As the coffee machine, almost an antique, warmed up he served himself some cereal and milk and thought about how someone could hack WIN. He drew some sketches in the spilt milk and then on the kitchen whiteboard. Ian frowned.

As the world's most authoritative source of information, WIN took great care over how information got into the system. Since the journalists and their associated cameramen, sound recordists and photographers were dotted all over the world; they had to send in their reports via a mixture of telecoms. Most came by satellite; others came in by the net. All of them were carefully authenticated against their origin. Several times.

When a journalist sent in his report, he would stamp it with a unique key composed of a retinal pattern, a security key and source locator. When the message was received the network sent a call back to the source locator to confirm the source and ask an extra question, the content of which changed daily and was known only to that journalist. This was not a normal, everyday question, but a digital one that only the receiving station could interpret correctly, in the presence of the journalist. It was designed to stop terrorists from forcing journalists to submit fake messages. And of course all the messages were heavily encrypted.

But somehow someone had got past the screen that Ian had built so carefully.

Fortified with coffee, he returned to the workspace and prepared for the conference call with the Permanent Network team. He was beginning to have an idea of what might have happened. But he'd need to have to see at least one more similar item to be sure. And he would have to go down to the WIN datacentre in London to check. This was not something he could do remotely.

When the call came in he was ready to answer the questions from Xavier and his colleagues. Instead he was amazed to see that Ashley Plank had joined Xavier at the meeting. That meant this was being taken very seriously. Ashley had been one of the three architects of the WIN authentication system, with Marc Spatz and Ian himself. Ian had gone on to be an independent operator, working on his own terms with WIN and others. Marc had gone off to work with other people with similar needs. Ashley alone had stayed on with WIN, and had risen through the politics to be Director of Networks.

Ashley was, as always, power dressed. Her smooth black, body-hugging outfit was the height of corporate chic. She always understood the importance of messages, both electronic and personal. Xavier Mann had learnt from her, and he was dressed in an ornate set of layers, in sharp contrast to Ashley's simplicity. Ashley looked at Ian's art T-shirt and running tights.

"Still running things your way, Ian, I see." she said to start the meeting. "Just as well, we're going to need some creativity to fix this one. Do you know what has happened?"

"Yes, someone has introduced a fully authenticated yet false, short life item." Ian replied, used to the sarcastic comment. "This is not the first one either, I've just checked the log for short-life items. There have been three this week, all minor political events. And nothing like that ever before."

"Good. I see you're more than keeping up with events. More than we can do down here surrounded as we are by corporate goodboys and yoyos. What do you make of it?" Ashley ignored Xavier wincing at her side at her description of WIN talent that probably included him.

"Very clever. I don't know how it has been done, yet. But I have a clue; maybe they have not been so clever. But I need to check out some other stuff first. I think I'll have to actually go to the secured zone to do it, too." Ian replied.

"Cute. When are you coming? I've a spare futon in my home space, want to try it?" replied Ashley. Xavier winced again, this was not how corporates are supposed to behave. When people did have to travel somewhere in the WIN management, they liked to stay in expensive hotels, not in other people's spare rooms. "And I'll join you down there too."

"I'm on my way, I'll call you when I arrive." said Ian, with a warm smile to Ashley, and then he dropped the link.

Ian's bedroom looked out the other side of the building, towards a series of depots and office. Many of them were disused, their forms softened by years of weather and plant growth. Trees pushed up through asphalt grids that had once held fossil-fuelled cars. Now most people could not afford to have their own vehicle. The running costs were too high, and with the Change the need to move long distances every day had been removed. Some people kept an electric buggy if they had to go to somewhere difficult to see family or friends, but most people just used taxis and communal transits.

Ian did not have a buggy, although he did have a bicycle. When he went anywhere it was a long way. For fun or for work, it meant several hours of travelling by fast means. Before the Change the air had been full of planes, burning fuel and filling the sky with noise. Now planes only crossed the big spaces of water, to the Americas, the Far East and the impossibly vast expanse of Russia and the former Soviet Union. Within Europe people travelled by rail runners, skimming along the old train lines fast, nearly silent, efficient and low polluting.

Without knowing how long he would be away, Ian instinctively started filling a worn suitcase. He put in enough stuff for a couple of weeks and several different climates. Better safe than sorry. He even put in a storm hat and dark glasses. Something felt odd about this trip.

He also took his portable work deck with him. A small version of the work wall and desk surface, this was a powerful but compact computer. Like the workspace it had network connections, but lower bandwidth over radio.

The apartment management system had already informed the building control computer that he was leaving for a while and the security screens were beginning to close. Smooth, hard skins on the inside of the windows, like eyelids closing on the wrong side. As Ian shut the front door he felt rather than heard the deadlocks engaging and a slight breath of air as the door pulled itself hard against the frame.

Despite having more electronics in the building than many large corporations, there was still a man watching the door. Ian told him he was leaving despite the fact that the guard already knew via the computers. In an age where communication happened over wires and fibres, the personal touch was all too rare. Ian knew that a couple of direct words, some thanks and a smile, would get better security than any amount of automated surveillance.

A request for a taxi had already been sent and when he left the old corporate lobby, now filled with contemporary sculpture, there was a buggy waiting to meet him. Based on chemical reactions, the buggy motors could run for hours and hours on a single power charge, but could not attain great speed. Somehow no matter how technology advanced it was unable to build cars that were both fast and environmentally efficient. So with the Change education had been used to alter people's attitudes. Educate them away from fast, sleek cars onto other values.

The taxi buggy trundled off towards the centre of the city. That had not changed, the great Victorian train sheds were lovingly restored, covering the rail runner platforms. Ian bought a ticket to London King's Cross, just as his great grandfather might have done. He took a business-class ticket, buying him a small office on the train where he could work undisturbed. After all, WIN would be paying.

two

Just over three hours later the rail runner arrived in London, at King's Cross Station in what had become Crossroads Village since the Change. Ian took a taxi directly over to the WIN Permanent Network centre, a discreet looking building in Portland Village. He did not like London, and resented having to be there. Even now that it was broken into a patchwork of villages, it was still a huge, messy city. As he rode through the streets in the back of the buggy he realised that it was five years since he had last been there.

Before the Change there had only been the very rich and the very poor who lived in the city. Now it was all mixed, with many former office buildings converted into dwellings. The happy cries of children heard again where once only grey masses of paper-pushing office workers had swarmed.

He paid the taxi driver and as he got out he wondered, as always, how this building had remained so calm on the exterior, when inside was the buzzing centre of a world of data. Behind the art-deco facade of expensively restored stone and its reproduction period windows lay an inner building. Steel and stressed concrete inside a soft glove of stone.

He entered the lobby to the hostile stare of the receptionist. No one outside of the corporate realms came here. Most people thought it was a rich dwelling house and walked on. Ian, in his personal attire, did not fit the image of corporate goodboy, and the receptionist did not like it.

"I'm meeting Ashley Blank", Ian said with a smile. "You'll find my security rating is fine. Very fine."

The receptionist ignored the smile and scanned Ian's identity card. As he had said his security rating was good. Very good, as good as the highest goodboy. The receptionist did not like this, but he tried to hide it behind a thin smile.

"I've put a call out for her," he intoned, "you might like to wait over *there* please."

However at that instant Ashley burst into reception and swept over to Ian, planting a kiss on one cheek. The receptionist could not cover his surprise, and shaking his head he returned to the mysterious business of all receptionists.

"How does it feel to be back in the big smoke?" Ashley asked using a name for London that dated back to before even the BBC.

"Terrible as usual. But I managed to get some useful work done on the runner. Do you want to know now?"

"Not now, come into my office, and maybe into the core. I suppose you're still addicted to that sludgy espresso stuff? Well I've got my old machine out of the cupboard for you." And Ashley led him through a set of period doors and into another world.

The few visitors that make it into the WIN data centre are surprised to see that the elevators have buttons numbering floors from one to ten. Outside the building clearly did not go higher than five storeys. The older members of the data centre team referred to it as the Tardis, after some ancient children's entertainment they had heard of from their parents. It is bigger inside than out, they explained in exasperation.

Of course the extra floors were cut into the ground, surrounded by an anti-bomb, anti-penetration and anti-electromagnetic well. Floors ten to five were in the basement, and one to four above ground. The lowest level, ten, contained the switching systems. Levels eight and nine contained more computer equipment, less sensitive than the switches, level seven contained environment control and other service equipment. Level six, like level ten, needed a key to get to it, and no one was entirely sure what was there. Level five was where the computer people, like Xavier, had their lightless offices.

In the other direction, the very top floor of the external building was hollow, containing nothing but communications devices pointing up to the sky. Access to the roof floor was strictly controlled, with several steel doors and, it was rumoured, a round-the-clock team of Ninjas watching the neighbourhood for possible intruders.

The Ninja's were folklore, being the code name for an electronic surveillance device with passive restraint capability. If someone did manage to pass the physical barriers to the roof, they would be reduced to quivering jelly by subsonics. The lower levels were no less secure. Even getting to the elevator Ian and Ashley had to pass through a full-height turnstile. Put your ID card into a box, it closes; you enter the mirror-glass turnstile, and recover your card from the other side. If your security clearance does not check out you remain locked, harmlessly, in the gate until the security team comes to remove you.

Although at her level of director Ashley could have had an office above ground, she opted to stay in the depths, where her team worked. Her small space was covered in notes, books and a splatter of different computer media; some so old they would have interested an archaeologist. A collection of pictures and cards stuck up around the walls, including a fading picture of her, Ian and Marc on the day WIN went live. Ian had the same photograph pinned up in his kitchen.

Ian spent a few minutes taking in Ashley's clutter to try and see, as he always did, how she could put up with the yoyos she had to work with. Nothing, her junk looked just the same as his. Some twentieth century art, some contemporary, restaurant cards from around the world, and the picture of the three of them. And a new one: a small girl smiling out from under blond curls.

"Who's the girl?" Ian asked.

"My niece" Ashley replied without looking up. "At last one of the Plank clan has hatched. My parents are delighted, they thought it would never happen." And she sighed. "Have you got anyone?" she asked out of the blue.

"No," Ian replied. "I've kind of given up for the moment. I've been doing a big contract and not thinking about it. What about you?"

"London is full of scum, swim in it long enough and some sticks." Ashley replied, and changed the subject. "Let's go make some coffee."

As they walked down the corridor she turned to Ian and smiled. "I think this may be more serious than you imagine, in your flippant little world of bits. We have to be careful; this is more than treading on people's toes. There is a lot at stake, so we're going to talk somewhere where they are not likely to be listening."

"Your office is bugged?" Ian exclaimed, "You must be really important! Can't you see who is bugging from the systems? And fix it?"

"If I fix it, I'll be under more scrutiny. It will attract attention. Pretending to be naive means I have more liberty. I took the precaution of putting the old espresso machine in a storage room where no ever goes. There are no bugs, I checked, so we can talk safely there."

As they dug out the machine from a carton, loaded it with water and set it in motion, Ian outlined his ideas about how the bogus news was working its way into WIN.

"First thing I noticed was that each news item had a short life, like some kind of test packet. They were coming onto the ship list and vanishing before most people noticed them. They were unlucky this morning as it happened to hit the prime get-up radio ship. Someone is going to be unpopular. I wonder how it happened.

"The other thing I noticed was how each item claimed to come from different journalists in different places. Yet the routing said they all came from the same internal network switch. I checked while I was on the runner, looking back through the log and confirmed my suspicion. Those packets should have come from different switches, but they did not."

"But how did they get into the system in the first place?" interrupted Ashley.

"I'm not sure, but I've got an idea. It's crazy though. I'm not going to tell you as you'll laugh. Not until I've the proof." Ian replied. "I need to look at the switches themselves, hardware and software. How do we get down to the Bowels?"

The Bowels was the computer team's name for the lowest levels of the centre, where all the collection and redistribution systems were located. Most people thought they used the name because the tenth underground level was the bowels of the earth, but that was not right. Those who knew better understood that the bowels are a very efficient system for extracting some of the most valuable elements from a lot of junk, and compacting the rest into a manageable form.

Protected in all directions from attack, the Bowels could generate their own power, and scrubbed their air when humans entered into them. The only links to the outside world were a small stair well and a glass tube containing a thick bundle of fibres up to the roof cluster of aerials. Glass with strands of copper in it, carefully arranged to make it completely secure. Drill into it and it breaks or shorts the wires. Crack it and the same thing happens. In fact any unwelcome attention could be detected and the alarm raised.

"Hmm. Even my security does not go down that far unchecked. What do you want to do down there?"

"Check the switch code." Ian looked at her directly. "Remember the parts we all inspected and sealed away from the switched data? The one we had a friend check in return for a few nice meals and some fine wine as we didn't trust the yoyos? I need to check it."

"You'd better be right", Ashley said after a pause, "I'll have to call Shiguru Osawa. His title is our security manager, but he prefers people to think of him as the enforcer. I think you'll like him. He doesn't give shit for protocol or status. He just likes things to be safe, calm and predictable. Pretty much the opposite of you, in that respect at least. I also think he is honest and we can trust him."

The old coffee machine started to make bubbling noises. Ian looked at Ashley and said "How do you know we can trust him?"

"I looked him up in a very private file and he's clean. Clean as a whistle."

"Of course he would be, he probably looks after the security records. Besides, I thought you didn't do that kind of thing? It might attract attention." Ian riposted imitating Ashley's voice.

"Not if you are discreet," Ashley countered, looking down trying to avoid turning pink. "And we don't have any choice. Only he can authorize access to the Bowels. I think your sludge is ready."

Later in the day Ashley took Ian to the Security floor and into Shiguru's office. His glass partitions looked out over a couple of men watching screens. He felt better that way, although most of the screens showed the results of the intelligent personnel tracking systems, not video.

Shiguru had been raised by Japanese parents in Europe. They had been on holiday when an earthquake had destroyed their home, and they never returned to Japan. They had settled in the Frankfort Business Village, working as efficient financial controllers. They had had two children, a girl and a boy. Shiguru was younger, and had grown up surrounded by financial and physical security. One day his sister Tinka had not returned from work on time, and he had gone across the park to find out why. What he discovered changed his life.

In a dark, drug-induced fit someone had entered the Business Village Shared Work Space and started throwing herself around. Equipment had been smashed and several people hurt. There were dark stains on the carpet and emergency services looking over figures wrapped in healing blankets. When the crazy reached Shiguru's sister's work area, she met more than her match. With calm and deliberate action Tinka had turned and temporarily paralysed her in one movement. When Village Security arrived they wanted to know what Tinka had done, and had to wait for the effect to wear off before deciding out what to do with the women.

What profoundly changed Shiguru's world was something different. It was the sudden realisation that the crazy woman should have been neutralised before she had done any damage, preferably on entering the building. With his parent's help he had developed a business around providing that kind of special security. Security so good that nothing unexpected could happen. Corporates liked that kind of predictability.

Shiguru also understood image. Although he charged a very handsome fee for his special services he always wore plain black clothes, with a small leather pouch on his belt. Most people believed he carried throwing stars in the pouch, but as only a few special people know, the pouch contained a message terminal. In Shiguru's planned system throwing stars would never be used, the rings of safety would stop any potential intruders. Should he need it he could survey and command the entire state of the building from the terminal, away from the security centre, alone if need be.

———————————

When Ian entered Shiguru's work space he was aware of a huge presence. What he saw was a solid man with plain, black clothes. So plain they had to be expensive, so expensive they had gone through fashion and out again into timeless basic style. A steady regard followed him and implied that he should sit down. Ashley started her best goodboy act.

"Don't waste your time Ashley Plank," replied the security man, "or mine. I don't like yoyo speak any more than you. What do you and your friend want?"

"I need to go to the sealed switch rooms on the tenth floor." stated Ian. "I was one of the original architects of the switching system, and I believe their integrity has been impaired. I can only check this by looking at the closed system."

"'Integrity has been impaired'? What do you mean? You've discovered a prehistoric bug or someone has been fiddling? If you're trying to tell me the latter, I can only say that the last time anyone entered that level was more than five years ago."

"Five years or five hundred. Does it matter?" Ian answered, and was rewarded by a slow smile. "What happened five years ago? When we sealed up those rooms everything was specified to have fifteen years of operation."

"It says here," replied the security man looking at a display built into his desk, "that someone entered to check the air flow on one of the switch umbilicals. An environment sensor had reported that the flow was reduced."

"Can you tell me which switch?" asked Ian, with rising excitement.

"Not immediately, but I can tell you that the environment sensors are located outside the sealed area." Shiguru looked straight at Ian as he said this, making him feel that this quiet man had already deduced everything.

"I think it is time for more coffee," said Ashley, watching the man in black closely. "We pulled out an old machine in one of the store rooms for Ian." Again the slow smile and a tiny nod of comprehension.

"I always prefer a fresh espresso to the machine stuff," replied Shiguru. "However it is a little too late in the day for strong coffee, for me at least. In return for your kind offer, I'd like to invite you to dine with me in a special place."

"We would be honoured," Ashley said, "where would this special place be?"

"London may have changed greatly since the turn of the century, but there are still private clubs. I have the good fortune to be a member of the Nippon-Su club. This is my card, it tells you the address, and will also allow you to enter. Be there for nine."

"In that case we are *most* honoured, and delighted to accept." Ian said.

three

After meeting with Shiguru, Ashley and Ian left the WIN building and walked the short distance to Ashley's apartment. Ian expected it to be in much the same style as his own, but was surprised to see something completely different. Forming the top floor of an old office block, she had used huge surfaces of natural wood, linked by twisted glass inserts. Breaking up the walls were bright posters of late-twentieth century art, including some stuff that had shocked when first displayed, but had blended into the art world with time.

Light seemed to diffuse into her main living space from all round, and she explained that she had installed a light catching system on the roof that diffused the evening sun in through light ducts and flowed out into the room. "It's like air conditioning for the eyes," she explained. "When the sun goes down it uses artificial light to maintain a good level of ambient light."

"Sounds expensive," Ian said.

"To install, yes, but cheap to run. After all, *I* don't have a Plomb'Art bathroom." Ashley countered, and they both laughed.

"I'm never going to make it until nine without eating," Ian said, "have you got anything I can nibble?"

"Sure, the fridge is that way. This is not a personal remark, but you might like to inspect the work of the Natural Washing Company. They've just finished remodelling the main bathroom. Not as sophisticated, arty or expensive as Plomb'Art, but quite pleasing none the less."

The Nippon-Su club was a couple of villages away from where Ashley lived, so they took a buggy over there. Being careful to be on time, they arrived outside a very plain building, with two large Japanese men standing protectively on either side of the door. They wore plain, old-fashioned suits that fitted tightly over large muscles.

As Ian and Ashley approached the door of the club they started to move to block the entrance. A sight of Shiguru's card changed that.

"Welcome to the Nippon-Su," said one of the bouncers, "our premises are entirely at the disposable of close friends of our members. The staff inside will make sure your needs are seen too."

Inside they were met by a serious young lady who led them through the club to a quiet dining room. Carefully furnished in 1980s Milan design furniture, beautifully restored, the room contained only a few tables, discreetly spaced so that guests' conversations could not be overheard. Shiguru had chosen well, especially since he saw to it personally that there was no unwanted surveillance of the front door.

Their host was waiting at a table for them. He rose to his feet, shook hands, and waved them to sit down.

"First we will eat." Shiguru said. "You are hungry, Ian. I can tell. Because of the way you work you're all nerves and brain activity. Your energy balance is off. You don't do enough sport, and your metabolism is all out of alignment. Ignoring all the old vocabulary of energy centres, chakra point of ying and yang, you need more balance in your life. Please excuse me for being so direct, but I think you appreciate that."

"I do, and I thank you for it." Ian replied, "And may I add that you are one of the most observant people I have ever met, with an astonishing capacity for synthesis."

"I was trained to put things together", Shiguru answered. "My parents put great importance on understanding systems and the way they function. You look at great information systems; I look at people systems. There are many similarities, but the skills to work them are quite different. Ashley combines some of both, which is most unusual. She also understands the importance of her work, which is why she stays here, to stop the yes-people taking over and destroying the structure that gave them life. Stopping the implosion."

"You too, Shiguru", said Ashley. She had never heard anyone explain so well why she stayed, battling with hierarchy-driven idiots on a daily basis. "You are most perceptive, which is what Ian

19

was trying to say. Since the Change most companies have broken into tiny units, and there is less need for the middle layers. WIN is one of the few companies that are still that large, and unfortunately needs to be that way to function. Even I find it hard to explain it, but I feel a deep dedication to what we have built."

"What do you want to eat? We can resume the self-congratulatory discussion later." Ian said, laughing. "You're right about my metabolism. And it's beginning to manifest itself!"

"Around your middle?" asked Ashley, her turn to laugh.

————————

The Nippon-Su provided several different menus for its members and their guests. Shiguru had chosen one that consisted of simply prepared fish dishes, from different places around the world. But the ingredient balances were perfect. "We have serious things to discuss," he said, putting the wine list to one side, "so I'm afraid we shall have to do without the pleasures of the vine."

When they had finished eating they took their tea bowls to a sitting area, this time decorated in classic club style. Settling into heavy leather winged chairs, again discreetly grouped to allow private discussions, Shiguru started to speak.

"WIN takes in a huge trawl of news and filters and sifts it. We pride ourselves and demand high prices for the accuracy, completeness, and of course speed, of our news feed. We are so good that we have no serious competitors. Our customers buy news to know what to do with their huge wealth, or to disperse it to a public audience, large or small.

"Last century there were several terrible wars, and during some of them it was proposed that the enemy's water supply should be polluted. This would kill huge numbers of people and stop industry. This was never done, or not on a large scale, although many other horrors happened.

"From the looks on your faces, I see that someone is trying to pollute our news supply. They are, somehow, adding poison to our reservoir and we will unwittingly ship it to our customers. This will cause devastating financial instability and could cause massive public morale problems, even leading to public disorder. Am I right?"

"Almost," said Ian, "what we are seeing is the poison being added after we have filtered the water flowing from the reservoir. It is as if someone has entered the water treatment building and added poison to the other chemicals. Fortunately they have just been making little tests, and have not done anything serious."

"So we can hope that our customers have not noticed that our produce is not up to its usual standard." Shiguru continued. "Assuming for the moment that the polluters are not wanting to wipe out the whole population, they are targeting industries. By poisoning the news they can destabilise certain companies?"

"Yes," explained Ashley, "by choosing different types of false news they could conceivably target different types of company. Most of our business customers have built automated systems which make business-critical decisions - sorry for the yo-yo speak - automatically. For example a chemical company could be seriously perturbed by false news of a strike of its third-world workers. The fact that the company would, in theory, be the first to know of the strike does not matter as the news is flowing through different departments.

"Equally, the false news - good or bad - could apply to a competitor. Or like this morning's plant, a political event could be used to target financial markets. The theory says that most investors do not like political extremists. This dislike manifests itself in the form of selling stock to buy more secure investment options. So if we ship out a political win for an extremist, then the banking buy-sell systems set off to transfer money from at-risk shares to safe investments. Automatically."

"And given we sell our news worldwide, that can happen anywhere, and round the clock," concluded Shiguru. "So why did that not happen this morning?"

"Ah, I checked that," Ian said. "There is a delay of fifteen minutes from receiving a news item before shipping it to business users. Our news-delivery customers demand to have some competitive advantage other than editorialising, so every item goes straight out to the media as soon as we receive it. News going to businesses waits for a few minutes before shipping. As the test items have a very short life - five minutes in this case - they have as yet to be shipped to businesses."

"So how do the messages get in after the filtering and sorting stage?" asked Shiguru.

"Well, I have a theory." Ian said. "But I need to check it. Your news that the environmental systems had to be checked five years ago gave me an insight. One thing I don't understand is why the environment control equipment is so much closer to the surface than the machine rooms."

"I can explain that," said Ashley, "it's because the chillers need both air and drains. When the air conditioning systems are working, water condenses inside the chiller, and that must be fed out to the normal drains. Similarly there are air ducts bringing fresh air into the plant."

"Good!" exclaimed Ian, "My theory is confirmed. Since the Bowels are electromagnetically sealed, there must be some kind of cable coming into the building carrying the information. This is reinforced by the fact that the false items are coming only from one switch, the one with the cable. What I could not understand was how a cable - probably a fibre - was brought in.

"So my theory is that when the environmental umbilical was repaired, someone pulled a fibre through from the drains, to the chiller, and then down the umbilical to the switch. Fibre can run up to twenty-five kilometres with no signal loss, so the other end of the link could be quite far away.

"But to do all of this requires a few more things. One is the technical knowledge to be able to quickly modify the switch code to listen to the wire; another is access to repair the system. How could that happen?"

Shiguru frowned. "Almost anyone can get into the environment control rooms as they require regular servicing - mechanical systems being what they are. Funnily enough I checked through with Permanent Network and the person who performed the repair five years ago is no longer there. In fact she only worked for them for a few months, but was, apparently, very good. I have her picture on the system. Tell me, what kind of person would have that technical knowledge?"

"Someone like Ian," Ashley replied, "a software archaeologist. Contrary to the clean, systematic image we like to put about, software is messy and organic. Bits of code are added here, there and everywhere. No plan. It's like a mediaeval village: if you need another room on your house you just build it. Organised - sometimes - chaos. It is very easy to create monstrous, unmanageable systems, and then people like Ian have to go through and work out what is happening. However with our code that would be quite easy, as we wrote some good stuff. It would not take long to figure out how to graft something on. After all, we designed the program with that in mind."

"It would still take someone extremely talented to figure out the change in the time available," Ian said, "It should not be too hard to find out who it was, as there is only one place that specialises in my unlikely line of work. It's Hackville, just outside of Paris in the old business district of La Defense. You can learn about all sorts of archaic computers and software there, and it's where most people work from too. Given the picture of our mysterious cyber plumber, we can maybe find her. I have many good friends there who can help me."

"You use the word archaic," Shiguru observed, "but I thought we at WIN offer a world-class service. How come we use old machines?"

"Quite simply because they were known to be reliable," explained Ashley. "New things break, especially software!"

"So what do we do next?" asked Ian.

"Well, I think this may be much more serious than you think. Many unexpected things could happen." Shiguru said seriously. "My life is dedicated to making sure unpleasant surprises do not happen. I think the best approach is for me to speak to some friends and arrange for your mysterious fibre to be traced. Assuming it exists. I'd prefer that you, Ian, keep away from the environmental controls to avoid raising alarms. However I think you should go to the Bowels and check the code."

"That's fine by me," Ian agreed. "But this is not going to be like tracing a cable through some old installation. Not even like tracing some crazy old phone system. This is going to be well hidden and go some interesting routes. With cases like that most people just cut the ends off the cable and lay a new one."

"Don't worry, my friends are good at following wires through interesting places." Shiguru replied calmly, "Just as you are the best in your area, Ian, these people are the best in theirs. When they find the other end, if it exists, they will call you and you can come along and do whatever software stuff you need to do. I guess, somehow, that will not be the end of the trail."

"And the cyber plumber?" asked Ashley.

"I think Ian may have to visit Hackville to find out about that." Shiguru answered. "But I have safe friends in Paris who can help. Ashley, you recently ran a security check on me through my own systems. You did it very well, with a lot of skill. But how do you know it is true, and why do you trust me?"

"You've some smart systems there," Ashley said in awe, "I had no idea you'd picked me up. As for trust, we don't seem to have much choice, do we? We need to get to the Bowels, and coming directly to you seemed the only route. We have no experience of breaking and entry, even if we could break in down there. I hope that we can trust you, because I too share your fears of the scope of this thing."

"I hope I am worthy of your trust then. I think it best if we do not meet in the WIN office again. This is my personal number," said Shiguru passing them each a card, "call me or drop a message if you want help or need to meet. I already have your personal numbers.

"Tomorrow you will have access to the Bowels, Ian. Your ID will be enough to let you in. Try and come in early and avoid letting people see you. Head for Ashley's office on entering, and then go down. Again, please be careful. From what you have told me the people we are investigating are patient and powerful. That usually means dangerous."

"Do you have an idea, then, of who might want to do this?" asked Ian.

"There are always difficult people about. Perhaps a competitor, perhaps organised crime, or perhaps a government. Since we have no serious rivals we can discount competitors. We are certainly a problem for certain governments who like to keep their peoples ignorant, but they do not usually plan so far in advance. Governments have a short-term focus on the next election. Unfortunately I think it is most likely to be some large criminal organisation.

"Whatever you do with the bits down there, make sure you don't disrupt the flow, or we will never get to the end. Any indication that we have noticed the change and we're lost. And that might mean more than safeguarding the information network."

Shiguru's reply did not make Ashley or Ian feel any happier about what they were doing. But they both felt a sense of adventure and excitement they had not felt for years.

four

Ian arrived at WIN shortly after seven the next morning. As planned, he went to Ashley's office and checked his messages. Shiguru had been working through the night, and his mail contained the ID of the switch that had been modified, a picture of the mysterious woman who had come to repair the chiller, and information about someone called Bruce who was going to follow the wire.

Ian found his hands sweating when the ID of the modified switch matched that of the source of the rogue messages. Excitement and a feeling of fear flooded him. The last time he had felt that was when he'd been biking in a canyon bottom and twisted his ankle so that he could barely walk, let alone pedal his bike. But he'd put his swollen ankle in the cold water of the stream and had made it out. This time he needed to plunge into the stream of information, and follow the bits to where they came from.

The missing cyber plumber had the face of a young, arrogant hacker. She was wearing a Permanent Network service outfit, but she had a very personal hair cut. Normally contractors followed conservative corporate styles to the letter. One side of her hair was grown long, and the other cut short and sticking up. All the hair was coloured bright red. The picture showed one earring with a lightning bolt hanging from the exposed side. She had a nice smile. Ian was nervous of nice smiles; they could lead to all sorts of trouble.

The mail about Bruce revealed he was a real cyber plumber, a specialist in cables and pipes, with the unusual feature of working on undocumented systems. Sometimes networks grew organically too, like a coral reef, layer on layer, year on year. He was good at following cables and fibres to their sources. In fact he was the best. The mail also recorded that he was an Australian and had a number of other pursuits, including caving and martial arts. An extra note on the biography stated that his name really was Bruce, and that he did not appreciate jokes about it.

Working from the chillers out, Bruce had apparently already started in the middle of the night. He had sent Ian a message confirming that a fibre left the chiller via the drip channel, into the drains. He was following it, via the sewers and various gadgets that helped him track the path through the smaller ducts. His mail said he would soon have to stop and would start again at night. He'd send more mail when he had got further.

Ian took his work deck and a big bag of connectors with him. Most machines used wireless connections these days, but the old switches needed a cable to connect them to his deck. In the lift he had to select level ten, which actually took him to a level between nine and ten, deep in thick concrete.

Only his special security status from Shiguru let him get this far, and he still had a few steps to go before getting to the stairs. He put his palm on a reader, and was approved. A scanner checked he was alone, and the first door unlocked. Inside the next door would not open until the first had shut and locked. He imagined the mysterious hacker coming down here on her mission to add extra code to a system she had probably never seen before. She must have been even more worried and frightened than he was, but not much.

Another scan checked that he was alone in the space between the two massive doors. With a thud of heavy bolts and a hiss of air pressure the inner door opened to reveal a small metal stairwell, descending into a large room full of anonymous machines. Ian remembered working here for hours and hours, losing all track of surface time. As he walked between the machines their layout came back, and he walked up to the switch that had been infiltrated. It looked just like the rest: the pale cream colour computer companies call grey, a switch ID, a few indicator lights, and a small plastic key holding the front panels shut.

Nervously Ian unlocked and opened the panels, revealing more plates and neatly bundled cables. All the cables looked the same, so she had used identical fibre. The cable management had let her hook the fibre in so that you could not tell if anything had been changed. But Ian noticed a small asymmetry: all the sockets were in use, whereas there should have been one spare.

Opening the cabinet behind him he confirmed that it had fifteen cables and one spare socket. The one in danger had sixteen cables. He looked carefully at the connectors and there was a minute difference in the sixteenth.

He pulled out a cable from his bag and plugged in his work deck and was soon lost in the bits. Software archaeology is like mapping an ancient city, there is no plan to follow other than the vistas you see. You can follow one path or another, sure that they will cross later, and lose yourself in the baroque structures someone has created.

In this case however, Ian was doing something new. He was looking at code he had written some time before and looking for changes. He could check the modification dates on the programs that ran the switch and see what was different. He was disappointed, and found that somehow she had managed to reset the dates; however the sizes of three of the source code files were not as he expected. He plugged into the next door switch to check the sizes: he was rewarded. She had changed three key files and he could see which. Better, using his deck he could automatically find the differences.

He copied both the changed and original files down onto his system to work on them elsewhere. It was a bit disconcerting being down there on his own, with just the machines. Ian began to wonder what would happen if Shiguru was not trustworthy, and decided to get out of the machine room as fast as possible and head for somewhere more populous.

Unplugging from the two open switches, he locked the front panels and walked back to the stairs. Ian was slightly afraid that he would not be able to leave, but the doors opened for him, and he found his way back to Ashley's office.

"I've bad news for you," Ashley announced, as they made coffee in the safe storeroom. "And a tiny bit of good news."

"Oh. And I'm sad to say my guesses were correct. So this is as bad as Shiguru thinks. Tell me the worst news first." Ian replied.

"Ok. The worst is that you're going to have a 'colleague' working with you. Someone in the US has noticed and assigned a security consultant from Boston to come over and help." Ashley explained.

"So what is so bad about that?" Ian asked.

"Well she is well known for being a pain. Her name is Judith Planter-Smail and she comes from a rich family. She does not hide her opinions, so you should be all right."

"Well, tell me the rest of the bad and the good."

"Well remember the scum I mentioned? Well he objects to you being in my apartment. Sorry, you'll have to go to a hotel. The good news is that it is a very nice hotel, and that WIN is paying. Judith Planter-Smail is already booked into the same place."

"Hell, I suppose you've brought my stuff with your usual efficiency." Ian said. "I'll live, but he must be a real pain this man. Hasn't he heard of friends and spare rooms?"

"I'd really prefer not to talk about it, it's all too tedious. It's a long story." Ashley offered. "Yes, I have your stuff here. The hotel is in this village and is called the Crichton Court Private Hotel. Here is a map."

"Thanks, I'm off to the hotel then, to look at what Red was up to." Ian replied, taking the map.

"Who's Red?" Ashley asked.

"I've decided to call our mystery hacker Red because of her hair. Shiguru sent me a picture." Ian answered. "How much do we tell this Judith person?"

"I was thinking about that," said Ashley, "and I've checked her security. She is clean, but I think being a bit careful with the truth would not go wrong. Painful she may be, stupid she is not. So you can't easily pull the wool over her eyes. With your talent for blurting things out, perhaps a cut down version of what is really happening would be for the best."

A few minutes later Ian entered the calm interior of Crichton Court. He felt out of place in his bright leggings, T-shirt and leather jacket. However the reception staff were all delightful and he felt more cheerful as he went up to his room, which was called Charlotte. He had discovered that really chic boutique hotels gave their rooms names, not numbers.

He slid his key into the lock and pushed. The door opened a crack and blocked, followed by a nasal American scream of "Back off, I'm armed and covering the door. One move and I'll blow you away."

Unreasonably quickly a strong pair of hands took hold of him, lifted him off the ground and pulled him back. Crichton Court was very concerned about guest security and privacy.

"What the hell is happening here?" Ian yelled at his invisible assailant. He could not move his arms. "I just checked in, I open my door, and I'm attacked from behind!"

"I'm sorry sir, but you appear to be breaking and entering, and a lady's room too." said a smooth, polite voice. "The police will be here in a minute."

"Now wait a minute, I just checked in and was given that room." Ian replied. "My baggage is on the floor, I've a key card in my hand, and the booking record in my pocket. Does it sound like I'm breaking and entering?"

"I'm going to release your arm and you're going to give me the booking record. Any other movement and I shall be obliged to restrain you more forcefully," conceded the voice from behind.

Ian produced the paper showing him as being the occupant of the room and held it out behind his back. The strong arms let go and Ian turned to find a huge man in a suit like that worn by the bouncers at Nippon-Su.

"I am most terribly sorry to have treated you like that sir," said the security man, "but I'm sure you appreciate the need for us to protect our guests. Apparently reception believes that you and the lady in this suite were to be sharing. Let us go to the front desk and correct the matter."

When they arrived at reception the hotel manager was there already. Ian wondered if the hotel had some kind of telepathy system by which the staff could send each other messages. However the reason became obvious: someone was complaining vociferously on the telephone.

"That wouldn't be Judith Planter-Smail in the room I was given, would it?" Ian asked the manager.

"Yes, how do you know that, Mr McAllister?" he replied, knowing who Ian was without having to be told.

"Because I am going to have to work with her, and I wondered if that was the origin of the problem." Ian explained. "And she has the reputation for being difficult."

"Miss Planter-Smail's father has long been one of our customers on his trips to London," the manager said avoiding Ian's comment. "It was only natural that she should stay here too. Oh dear. I wonder if you could talk to her for us, sir?"

"I've never met her, but I can try." Ian admitted. He took the receiver and, ignoring the stream of words coming from the other end, said "Judith, this is Ian McAllister from WIN here. I believe we have been mistakenly booked a double room."

He was rewarded by a stunned silence at the other end. He continued "I am arranging for another room for myself, and when that is sorted, perhaps you could join me in a public room for some tea and a discussion."

"Mr McAllister, I have never been so insulted in my life. How could such a mistake have been made? I hope it was not yours," said the angry American voice.

"It's Dr McAllister, but I prefer to be called Ian. I think it was your office in Boston that made the arrangements, so I have no idea how it could have happened. However we have a lot of work to do, so let us pass on to real problems."

"Dr McAllister you are direct to the point of rudeness. In the interests of WIN I will try and over look this occurrence. Shall we meet in one hour? That will give me time to calm down and you to unpack."

Ian looked at his small bag and wondered how much stuff Judith Planter-Smail had brought with her. He said "All right, let us meet in the hotel parlour in one hour," and hung up without waiting for a reply. "Now," he said to the white-faced receptionist. "Do you have any rooms with futons?"

Ian waved the crowd of porters, the hotel manager, the apologetic security man, and the receptionist out of the suite he had been allocated. He discovered that this hotel only had suites, all of them decorated in a particular style. His was all Japanese furniture and paper screens. He was relieved to find, however, that the bathroom was more like a normal hotel: marble and tiles.

Reassured by the level of security in the hotel, Ian felt safe enough behind the solid, locked door. Without bothering to unpack his bag, he settled onto a folded futon chair in the sitting room to look at the modified programs he had loaded onto his deck. When he looked at the differences that his computer found for him automatically he was amazed. Red was a master craftsman. The changes were written to blend in exactly with Ian's original program. The layout was identical, the choice of identifiers the same as his. Even down to the occasional sarcastic remark in the sparse comments. And the changes were minimal; an optimal solution of which Ian would have been proud.

He knew from Shiguru's information that she had been in the machine during working hours for only two and half days. Yet she had built an understanding of the code that would have taken someone from Permanent Network weeks or even months to learn. Ian figured that Red must have done what he had just done: down loaded the programs to a deck and worked over night for the two nights to have achieved it. Without sleeping, probably.

Ian was amused to realise that Red's talent made it easier for him to work out what she had done. Her modifications were such a good mimic of his own style that he could understand them immediately. What she had done was patch the switch to allow the machine at the other end of the fibre to access any packet of information as it arrived at the switches and was dispatched, as well as allowing a packet to be injected into the main news stream down the fibre. It effectively allowed whoever had built this link to spy on the inner workings of the network and when comfortable with what needed doing, start to add their own information.

That was the easy part of the operation, it just confirmed his guesses. Now was the hard part, to work out how the rest of the system worked and trace it back to the source. It was only by extraordinary luck that a test message had fallen on the breakfast time news ship, the rest of the trace was going to be much harder. Especially since Ian suspected that the source must be in a different time zone, as the only conceivable explanation of the error. However before that he had another difficult task to accomplish: speaking to Judith Planter-Smail and finding out what she was doing.

five

Tea was served in bone china cups with dainty, impractical handles. A plate of shortbread accompanied the drinks, and there were even silver tongs to serve them. A pot of hot water to add to the large-leafed Earl Grey mixed with little blue flowers as they drank, completed the tray. Ian and Judith were seated in the Crichton Court Hotel's parlour, full of strange, dark paintings, heavy furnishings, and small trinkets. Ian was sure that Judith would call them "home furnishing accent items."

"I am responsible for systems security in the US," Judith explained, "which includes both technical, process and human relations work. I'm not an expert in software; I am more familiar with corporate structures and how they become infiltrated. You may be able to find out how the code was changed, but I'm more interested in how come someone was sneaked into WIN past the most strict security in the business."

Judith was about the same age as Ian or younger, but wore a fussy floral dress with a high neck. Despite apparently good skin she wore a dusting of makeup and her hair was mounted in waves. Her waistline was cut generously making her look larger than she was, and the dress flowed down to below her knees where it ended in a lace trim. Plain brogues with low heels completed the picture. Appearing much older than she was, Judith was clearly neither a power dresser, nor someone who did not care about image. Ian suspected that she was deliberately avoiding classification, or at least avoiding drawing attention to herself.

"Please don't explain things to me in technical detail," she continued, "I trust you to do that. It's not that I won't understand, it's just that I don't need to know. You have an exceptional technical reputation, but I must say your records for working with the corporation read like a textbook on how the best engineers behave. Badly of course. So I will not encroach on your area, if you leave me to be an expert in mine."

"Sounds fine to me," Ian concurred. "I dislike companies, hierarchy, official status, all the stuff that goes with 'manager mentality.' Creativity cannot be fitted into a mould. It sounds like you are an expert at fitting in but observing. If that is the case, I can tell you easily what I would like to know from your end."

"You could put it like that," Judith replied. "My father was in government politics. He has retired now, but I learnt from him how people bend the rules. How to look for cracks, know the limits. Corporations are like governments, so the same games are played. Fitting in is not quite right; but you are right about observing. Remember the old conundrum about not being able to measure a system without changing it? Well, I try and minimise my impact on the group I am monitoring; to do that I have not to fit into a fixed category, but not to stand out. Anyway, although I will run my own work, please tell me what you think I should do."

"Well, someone has run a fibre into the WIN data centre." Ian continued. He imagined Judith's father as being one of the grim, unsmiling people he had seen at airports and stations, never a show of emotion, expecting others to follow naturally. "This is supposedly impossible, but like most impossible things, it has happened. The only feasible route has been taken, and taken with great skill. The key has been that somehow a fault report was entered for the environment control system for one of the switches. We don't know if there was a real fault or whether the whole event was staged.

"When the fault was reported, a cyber plumber who was also an expert software archaeologist appeared, apparently from Permanent Network, did some fine work, and then disappeared. She vanished from company records shortly after the job. I've taken to calling her Red after her hair, as the name we have for her is certainly fake. I know, or think I know, how to follow the trail that we've found on to the next step at least, but we need to know how come she was called in."

"That was an admirable summary for a techy," Judith said without a trace of a smile. "I see why you are concerned. It is most unlike any building run by Mr Osawa to have such an event. I have heard much good of someone called Miss Plank. She sounds like a good start."

"Ashley Plank and I were two of the three original architects of the WIN information systems." Ian answered. "I know Ashley very well indeed, and I can tell you she will not appreciate being called 'Miss'. May I suggest you call her Ashley or 'Ms'?"

"Well that confirms that she was an engineer. I always prefer to be called Miss Planter-Smail, but I suppose you'll continue to call me Judith," Judith replied. "My father would not approve of such informality. If he knew about the rooms and you addressing me be my first name so soon he would be offended. Fortunately he is not here, and I have learnt to be more flexible. My family is as close to what you call 'old money' as you get in America. We have long traditions to uphold. However Ian, as you said you prefer to be addressed, tell me anything else you think I should know."

"Judith, I come from a family where only two things matter: how good you are, and respect for others," Ian countered. "Those are the values I learnt from my parents; that and our only tradition: never watching television. Well, we do all meet for a week of skiing once a year. What should you know? The only people I have spoken to so far are Ashley, Shiguru and now you. A Permanent Network contractor - Xavier Mann - also knows something is wrong, but I have not spoken to him since the first day we noticed something was wrong.

"The only other thing that you should maybe be aware of is that Shiguru believes that an organised crime syndicate is behind this scheme. That means it may be dangerous. All I can say is that the operation has been planned for a long number of years and has been very well executed until one day they slipped. They ran a news item so that it hit breakfast coverage in the UK. Perhaps that means that they are not in this time zone. Beyond that we don't know."

"I have been reading about this kind of operation," Judith said, "on the aeroplane over here, and had concluded that it must be some kind of criminal organisation. As I intend to be as discrete as possible, I am not worried. You, however, may have to expose yourself to danger. Your recorded behaviour leads me to believe you would not react well. Can I ask you to be most careful?"

"How do you work out my behaviour will be a problem?" Ian asked. "Because I argue with people?"

"Frankly, yes." Judith replied with a bluntness that Ian had not anticipated. "When told to do something you usually rebel. That may not be smart with organised crime; they expect obedience and discipline. Not two of your strong points, I fear."

"Well, I appreciate your concern, but I hope it will not come anywhere near that." Ian answered. "I hope we can leave all that to the police. Now, however, I must go back to work. Ashley will still be in the office if you want to go and meet her."

The next stage of the operation for Ian was to work out what might be at the other end of the fibre. What would be shipping information into the WIN switches. He figured it would be some antiquated computer system, sitting in a machine room belonging to some company, lost amongst large systems. The perpetrators would have some influence in that company, or even own it outright, and could easily manipulate the management information systems people.

In a fit of fantasy he imagined that some minor operative in a bank or insurance company would receive a small data block in the mail, electronic or physical, and have to put it into the rogue machine. They would not know what was happening, and would think they were being good corporate citizens, hoping for promotion and not asking questions.

In the middle of this reverie he received the call from Bruce the cyber plumber. It was early evening and it was getting dark in the street. Ian had expected more time, including time for dinner; he was beginning to get hungry again. Bruce's face appeared projected above Ian's work deck.

"Hi Ian, I've found it," Bruce announced. "Not quite what I had expected. Quite a surprise actually. These guys are too cute for words."

"What do you mean?" asked Ian.

"The best way for you to find out is come down here, now, and I'll take you in. We'll need you there to look at the computers or whatever's in there too." Bruce said cryptically. "Now do you know where Tower Hill tube station is?"

———————

Ian followed Bruce's directions down into the tube station. He arrived at the foot of the escalator to find the long-legged Australian waiting for him, accompanied by someone in London Underground uniform, a large yellow torch in his hand. Ian shook hands and asked which direction they were taking.

"Down the middle," Bruce said, laughing, "you see this metal door here? It leads to a series of service tunnels, including some access holes to the drain system. Our friends are well connected, because they came in here first. This is Bob, he works for the tube and is my usual guide when we go caving. Some of these tunnels are so old no one remembers where they go.

"Sometimes they can be quite fun. Full of strange old machines, mysterious draughts, rats, or even time traps."

"Time traps?" asked Ian.

"Well, when they built these tunnels they had to do all sorts of extra work in and around the basic structure." said Bob, speaking for the first time. "Sometimes the small service tunnels have deep shafts running directly down from them. For safety these were covered up with thick wooden panels. With time these have rotted - stand on them and you fall through into whatever is underneath, probably to your death. To make it worse, the floor is so thick with dust you can no longer tell stone, concrete or wood apart."

Bruce and Bob seemed to find this quite amusing, especially, it seemed, looking at Ian's face after he heard this. Without saying anything else they unlocked the metal door and walked into what was a clean, well-lit service tunnel. After a while numerous side tunnels started to appear, some of which had dank still air, others blowing warm air into their faces. None of the side tunnels were lit, but they all had names like roads.

After a while they turned into a smaller side tunnel, which Bob was mysteriously able to make light up. Ian spent some time looking for switches, then realised that they were so heavily painted over that they were now flush with the wall. A small yellowed plastic rocker appearing amidst a sea of thick-yellowed paint.

The new tunnel was slightly dusty, with quite a few footprints, and it had a strange smell. Bruce explained that this tunnel gave access to one of the large drainage merging points, where several large sewers met. A filtering system removed much of the floating debris, but it was very old and needed a lot of manual operation. A few minutes later they emerged in a large chamber full of the noise of water. The sewers poured a huge stream of water into a big bowl, where it span round and drained out down into a deeper, larger system.

Along the roofs of the tunnels was a profusion of cables of all kinds. Ian recognised some ancient multi-core copper cables, as well as many more fibres like the ones they were following. There were also a couple of large tubes bundled in with the wiring. Bruce noticed Ian's enquiring eyes looking at the tubes.

"That's a truly secure network," he explained. "It's a pneumatic system, air pressure pushes shuttles back and forth. You put your message onto paper, or a data block, or even a fine chocolate for your mistress, load it into the shuttle, drop the shuttle into the system and whoosh, off it goes to the other end. Pushed by compressed air. It's a very old technique that is coming back into its own now, as it's completely impossible to tap. With all the sophisticated electronics we have we can listen to whatever traffic is running on wires, fibres, microwave links, anything. But paper or datablocks in tubes we can't do. Because the tubes are kept under pressure any compromise is automatically detected."

"I've seen that in old films," Ian commented. "They used that system in shops to move money back and forth. I had no idea any one still used it."

"Only the very rich and the very paranoid," Bruce replied. "Most of the old systems have fallen into disuse, but governments still hang on to them."

"What about crime syndicates?" asked Ian.

"Not normally," Bruce replied. "It's too easy to see both ends and work out who is talking to who. Governments don't care about that stuff, but the Mafia and the triads sure do."

They made their way round the sewer chamber, and went down a short side tunnel. Unlike the others this one had metal doors embedded in its sides, and a cable rack on the roof. Thick bunches of cables fed down above the doors, which had labels so old it was hard to make out the marks. "BT", "AT&T UK", "Mercury", "West EuroBell" and others. One door had no marks but heavier locks than the others; it also looked very slightly different. Bruce paused in front of it, checking the cables.

"This is definitely it," he announced after a while.

"So what is so cute about it?" asked Ian.

"It's been aged," Bruce explained. "The door has been made to look like it is as old as the other service cupboards round here. But it is not, it's much newer. They have also made it look a lot less secure than it is. Ageing can be used to put off thieves, but making something look less secure, well, that must have been to put people like us off the trail."

With that he started to examine the locks. After them he looked with painstaking detail all round the edge of the door. He ran some instruments over the metal surface.

"This is it, and it looks like the door is safe," Bruce announced. "I'll have to fiddle the locks a bit to get it. Can you guys keep back in case there are some defence features that my gizmos can't detect."

After a few minutes of fiddling with a lock gun and some strange tools the mechanical locks fell opened. That left two electronic locks, one coded and one with a card swipe. Bruce pulled some more instruments from his bag and set to work. The swipe was apparently easy, he ran a card with a large ribbon of cable trailing from it to a black box just twice to undo the catch. The code was harder, but within five minutes it too was undone.

Bruce called them over and pulled the door open. Nothing happened except the light inside coming on. Ian looked in to see some elderly but reliable computer systems, a bunch of wires, power and environment control. Nothing else, no security systems. There were no screens or projection systems, so Ian plugged his deck into the back of the machine with another cable from his bag. Soon he was totally absorbed in what he found on the machine, and Bruce and Bob retired back to the sewage chamber to chat and watch the unlikely things that had fallen into the drains.

Ian was delighted to find that the machines were running an old operating system with which he was very familiar. He also knew the machine well too, and rapidly determined that as well as the fibre to WIN, there was a connection to the Internet. He checked, and there was no other means of getting data in and out of this cell, so it had to be that. He began to understand how the messages came in.

After a while Bruce appeared at his side and put a small paper cup of espresso down beside Ian and returned to the chamber. Ian absently drank the coffee as he dived into the bits. He found that the program style here was different, but still written by Red. Now he was trying to understand her way of working, just as she had had to do with his code. However Ian had an easier task at hand, he did not have to modify the system, although he discovered that it would be easy.

When Ian looked at the core of the program he felt his skin tingle, it was strange to see programming so like his own, but with a difference in accent. He found that it was a well-built system, easy to understand and modify. Now he understood how Red had made her modifications so quickly: they thought the same way.

Without really thinking about what he was doing he started to add an extra function to the program. It was so easy, and, he had to admit, he felt a challenge to do it. After all she had changed his software with grace and ease; he could do the same.

Bruce put his head round the door and saw that Ian was still absorbed. It was now late and the Tube would soon be closing for the night. Not that that was a problem. He was going to ask Ian how long he would be, but thought better of it, and returned to where Bob was waiting and discussed other ways out from the tunnels. They agreed a route and Bob left for home while the underground was still open.

Ian's little addition to Red's program was coming along nicely, and he had even imitated her style to hide the differences. He had no way of testing it, but the change was self-contained, and he felt confident that it would not break the rest of the system. He took a risk and installed the new version. To his relief nothing happened, meaning that all was well, at least for the moment. He knew Ashley would be mad at him for doing this, she always had been, but he liked to get new stuff out and in use.

After that he copied a number of different files from the computer down onto his deck so he could look at them later. Being an old system it was incredibly easy for him to pick up information from it without using fancy techniques.

He was astonished to discover his legs were stiff, his back ached, and he was desperately thirsty and hungry. He looked at the time on his work deck and was even more astonished. He walked out to find Bruce still waiting, his long legs folded round the railings above the sewage chamber. He was studying something that looked like a wiring diagram, but might have been a map.

"Sorry about the long wait," Ian apologised to Bruce, "they call that a computer coma. You no longer notice time, your surrounds or your bodily needs."

"I know about that too," Bruce answered, "except for me I get absorbed in following cables round tunnels or buildings. When I was younger I did my jobs in one go, without sleeping. It was a challenge, and I did it. Now I'm calmer about it, take my time. I don't know about you, but I could do with some food and drink. Does that sound good? I know where there are some interesting late night places where you'll find some things to eat like you've never seen before. Not to mention the drink, or the decor."

six

Ian slept long and late on his hotel futon. He was woken by a call. Without thinking he accepted it, to find himself facing Ashley.

"Hey, good job this is not a conference call." she commented, and he realised he was naked. "And besides, you need to lose some weight. Do you want me to call back?"

"Not if it's OK with you," Ian replied, climbing back into bed. "I forgot. At home I have the camera permanently off on all my phones except in the workspace. What do you want?"

"Shiguru tells me you were out on the town last night with Bruce. Did you do anything useful, or just go to dives?"

"Hell, you know me. I'm so dull I prefer working to clubbing. Anyway, I refused to go into the place he picked second time round!" Ian retorted.

"Well it's true you like work, but I'd not say you were that dull. Where did you go then?" Ashley asked with her mischievous grin.

"First we spent some hours in a charming underground bar which served up an interesting cocktail. I could tell you about it over coffee." Ian said, suddenly remembering that someone might be bugging them. He wondered what they would make of impeccably dressed Ashley talking calmly to this naked engineer. "Then he took me to the Drum & Mux which he told me was a pub frequented by cyber plumbers. It was pretty dull, I still don't like pubs, and there was no sign of Red or anyone like her. In fact they were all men. On the way back to the hotel he tried to drag me into some place called Cheetahs, which he said was interesting. That was enough to make me jump a buggy back to the hotel."

"Do you know what Cheetahs is?" Ashley enquired and Ian shook his head. "It's a strip joint, where you push money into the dancers' g-string and he or she wriggles around especially for you. My scum took me there one night, so I upset him by sliding some money to a hunky guy. He was kind of talented, and gave me my money's worth. We left shortly afterwards and I'm pleased to say we've not been back."

"Lucky escape then," Ian said. "Shall I come over to your office and we'll take some coffee?"

"Yes," replied Ashley, "but do put some clothes on first."

Down in the storeroom they met, but Ashley motioned not to speak. They moved the machine into another store.

"I checked and someone has added a new bug on that store room." Ashley explained.

"We should get Judith to look into that too. She's explained to me what she does. I suggested that she look into who could raise the fault on the environmental system in the first place." Ian said. "She'll be delighted to look into the bug."

"Sorry to disappoint your boy-scout enthusiasm, but the person who put the bug in was Shiguru. He warned me first, that way he covers himself. Besides, she and I had a different discussion. We're going to gang up on you and make sure you don't do anything silly, like changing the code at the other end of the fibre."

Ian did his best to hide his reaction to this, and hastily changed the subject. "Do you want to know what I found out last night? Well, it's so simple: they have a mail-activated server. It works like this: they send an Internet mail message to a given address. The mail contains the fake news item to insert, along with ship-list life, source and all the other stuff. The machine at this end packs it up and sends it down the wire to our switch, and off it goes into the news.

"The remote machine can do other things, like picking stuff up from our end and shipping it off to a remote address. Fortunately it was an old operating system, so I could get discarded files back off the disk. Rummaging around in them I found lots of old mail messages. That way I could get the address where the requests are coming from, assuming that is the end of the trail."

"So where is it?" Ashley asked.

"Looking at the Internet address it's somewhere in Paris, so I figure it is in Hackville. I need to go there anyway as I'm sure someone there will know Red, or at least know of her. I've examples of her own code now to show people."

"Nice for you. I've not been to Hackville for years. And I can't go with you this time either. I'll have to send Judith with you to make sure you don't do anything stupid. She has so far not lived up to her reputation for being difficult and snooty. She's been charming with me."

Ian did not mention the incident of the rooms, nor of his guidance on how to address her. He just said: "Ashley."

"Yes?"

"The machine Bruce found is called Scarlet."

Hackville was the old business district of Paris, La Defense. When the Change happened the big corporations moved out, leaving some spectacular buildings that were taken over by people like Ian and Ashley. They formed the largest community of computer specialists in the world. Hardware, software and network archaeologists, and other experts at breathing life into old and new systems.

The three most impressive buildings were at one end, around a huge concrete square. Unusually two of them had retained their original functions: a shopping complex, and the other a mixture of hotel and exhibition facilities. The last building was La Grande Arche, a soaring monument in concrete, a box with an internal space thirty storeys high. It had once been a mixture of government and commercial offices, but now it contained the apartments of the best and worst of Hackville. If you lived in La Grande Arche you were either one of the great names of all time, or you worked on the dark side, as a computer criminal.

The hotel-exhibit building had been the Centre National de l'Informatique et de la Technologie, or the CNIT, and much of it had remained unchanged. Under the huge spanning roof - the original purpose of the place had been a sports hall - was now a market. In the market people sold services and equipment. Some computers were so old only specialists could recognise them. Others sold strange connectors and cables, others programs on long-forgotten media. Piles of small plastic squares with a metal shutter on them abounded. Heaps of mouldy magazines contrasted with shiny new data blocks. Other stands sold services: data recovery, archaeology, programming, and the occasional more secret person not disclosing what they could do.

Like a medieval market there was a good supply of food and drink vendors mixed between the piles of junk or polished service counters. Microbars abounded, generally serving espresso and energy drinks. On warm days the market spread out onto the concrete plaza, and the bars would find chairs and umbrellas hidden away in some basement and bring them out.

However Hackville was only the visible part of the old La Defense. Under the concrete and the fountains once lay a complex, twisted network of roads, car parks and tunnels serving the rich underbelly of corporate life. With the Change this became useless, and did not attract the hackers. It was too dark, too ugly and did not have enough large open spaces for conversion.

A different type of community had formed; one that preferred the dark privacy of this underworld. So much so that even the openings that once carried cars and trucks had been built over, excluding the light and prying eyes of the outside world. Only the underground station was still open and connected to Hackville on the surface, the rest was dedicated to Bidonsol.

———

Ian arrived by rail runner in the centre of Paris, and took the metro out to Hackville. From the Crichton Court Hotel in central London it only took him three hours to arrive at the Hotel International de l'Informatique in the old CNIT building. He checked in and found his room as close to his own apartment as possible. There was a futon, a bathroom by Plomb'Art and all the different network connections he could use. There was even a darkened work area and a brighter living space. He was just glad that WIN was picking up the bill.

The room was completed by a sound system and a pod-based coffee maker. This place had been redeveloped to serve the

Hackville community. It was expensive, but WIN was still paying, and wanted him to be working at his best.

On the runner over he had worked out that he had three things to do. The first was to locate where the mail with the fake messages was coming from, the second was to find Red. He had a nagging suspicion that there was a third, but could not name it.

Shiguru had given Ian a reference for someone working at Bell South Europe. He had an interview fixed for that afternoon. After unpacking he headed back into central Paris to find the Bell South Europe office where he was meeting a Jacques Dupuis.

"Welcome to Paris Mr McAllister", said Mr Dupuis. "My friend Mr Osawa said I might be able to help you. Any friend of his will always have a welcome here. In what may I assist you?"

"Thank you, please call me Ian," he replied. "It is really quite simple: I'm looking for the physical location of an Internet address. Shiguru knows people who can do things like that in London, and suggested that you could find someone here. WIN will be paying as I am working for them."

"Ah, well in that case, Ian, I will allocate our best network explorer to the task. I'll ask her to come up," assured Mr Dupuis, turning to his telephone. After a short conversation in French he looked up again at Ian. "If Shiguru Osawa is involved in the affair, it must be something important and to do with security. I will not enquire what the matter is, but I must say to be careful. You are no longer in your own territory, and people may not just speak differently, they may work differently, and have different values to your own. I can assure you that the agent I have allocated you is totally reliable and trustworthy. You may wish to explain more to her than you would to me, but may I recommend you do not tell anyone else you meet about the affair."

Ian tried to imagine what Shiguru must have said to this serious man to make him give such a gracious warning. He had imagined another cyber plumber like Bruce, so when he heard that the person coming to help him was a woman, he had visualised someone similar. However nothing had prepared him for what happened. When the door opened he saw a woman of about his age, wearing

Bell South Europe overalls. As he stood up to shake hands their eyes met.

As Ian had told Ashley, it had been some time since he had thought about girls, but even before he had never felt anything like he felt then. It was obvious that she was feeling something similar. Ian's every nerve tingled and a flood of hormones burst into his blood stream. Their hands met and stayed together for much longer than a normal business introduction. He looked into her brown, calm eyes under short black hair, and she looked right back.

"Hi, I'm Ian McAllister, I need to locate a network address," he finally managed to say. "And I'm sorry, but I don't speak much French."

"My name is Zozo, and it's OK," she replied ambiguously with a smile, still holding his hand tight in hers. "What can you tell me about the address I must find?"

"I've only the Internet address, and I think it is somewhere in Hackville," Ian managed to say. "I can give you a data block with all the information, and my address too, so you can call me or mail me when you've found it."

"Sure," she replied. "Let's do that. There are still plenty of useful hours today."

Ian gave her the data block, she made the lightest touch on his arm, and left the room with a serious nod to Jacques Dupuis, and a secret smile to Ian. He collapsed back into the chair. Jacques looked at him quizzically but did not say anything. Finally he smiled.

"I think Zozo will already be tracing that location, and will not hesitate to contact you directly," he said after a pause. "I do not believe that I can be of much more use to you, so if you'll excuse me, I must continue with my work."

"Oh yes, of course," Ian said, still completely absorbed by the brown eyes. He realised that all he remember was her face and her eyes. He vaguely remembered that she had been wearing overalls, but no idea of her shape other than she was slim. "Thank you very much indeed for your help. I won't bother you again."

Ian left the building with the intention of returning to Hackville, to find his mentor, but all he kept thinking about was Zozo. He found great comfort in her calm eyes, but deep angst as to whether she would contact him just for the network address, or for him. Then he remembered her touch to his arm, and managed to regain some concentration.

The greatest of all software archaeologists was Bill Ackerman. He was an American, and had worked for all the great old names of the computer business: Digital, IBM, CDC, Sun. He had, more importantly, worked for all their major customers and sorted out more information tangles than anyone else. Bill had been Ian's mentor and teacher after he had finished university. Ian had worked as an apprentice on what Bill referred to as "bit digs". The older man now lived in Hackville in semi-retirement, and Ian figured he had to know who Red was. No one could learn to program antique systems like that without coming into contact with Bill.

As he rode from the Bell office out to Hackville, Ian put a call through to Bill's apartment to check he was there. To both their delights, he was, and Ian was ordered to come straight up, into one side of La Grande Arche.

"Come in my boy!" Bill called from inside the work space, as the security systems let Ian in. "I've moved into rather better space than where you were last. Did you know that Oracle used to use this floor? Rather appropriate, I thought. How much closer to a dinosaur's lair can I get? Tell me, then, apart from the pleasure of your company, to what do I owe your visit?"

"I have some mysterious patches to my old WIN code", Ian answered.

"So, that's perfectly normal," Bill replied.

"Not when the code is on machines that are isolated in a locked, secured room. And not when the patches are so perfect that they look like original. Also, I have some of her own code, and it reads like mine." Ian explained in a gulp; Bill was quick on the uptake.

"How do you know it's a girl?" he asked.

"I've an image of the person who did it as she entered the building. But it was five years ago. I thought the easiest way to identify her was to show you the code."

"I may be old," replied Bill, "but I'm still happy to see pictures of women! Show me this image, and then let us look at code if need be. I see code every day, after all. In any case, I think I know who it is."

Ian pulled up the picture Shiguru had sent him, and Bill nodded his head. "Yes, that's her. I had feared she had gone to the dark side; now you've confirmed my fear. When she was working with me she had normal hair, though."

With a sigh the older man sat back in his chair. "Her real name is Tamzen Shapiro. She likes to be called Rouge. She was good, very good. As good as you, Ian, and that is saying a lot. However she had strange ideas, different values. She thought that she should sleep with me as her supervisor, even though she knew I've been with Susan for as long as we can remember. I remember worrying that she could not tell good from bad, or rather did not care about the difference. She was only concerned about doing great works, and felt that justified all. She could be dangerous."

seven

Much later that night Ian could not get to sleep. His mind was filled with images of Zozo, her calm brown eyes, the touch on his arm. It was that image of calm combined with the hormone surge that got him. Lying in the strange hotel room he felt very alone, and regretted the years of being on his own.

Suddenly Ian was wide-awake. Always a light sleeper, the slightest noise could disturb him. He had heard a noise at the door. There was another noise, and the door started to open, letting some light in from the corridor. He had, of course, forgotten to put on the safety catch, and Shiguru's words of warning came back to him. All he could see was the light cast across the floor of the room from the corridor. The shadow of a figure blocked the light for a second and the door closed again. His whole body tensed up as someone came into his room, silently, and closed the door.

"Who is it and what do you want?" Ian said, trying to keep a calm tone. He found he had pulled the bed covers up around himself. Hearing his own voice high and thin with fear made him feel even worse.

"It's Zozo ... from Bell South Europe," came the reply. After a short pause Zozo continued "I ... needed to check that you were OK. I was worried in case that the bad guys had traced you. It's easy to find people."

She sat down on the edge of the bed and looked at him in the dim light. "Actually it's so easy to check on people that I even checked the hotel computer to see if you were checked in alone. It's a bit embarrassing. I felt like a teenager again."

Ian let out a huge sigh of relief. "Don't worry, I am currently checked into life on my own. Shall I put the light on? I want to see your eyes."

"My eyes? Yes, please do, I want to see you too." Zozo said. When Ian turned on the lights, he saw she was dressed in black leggings, and a black, body-hugging T-shirt. She dressed much as Ian did, except she wore black and, Ian noted happily, she was athletically

51

built. Neither too thin nor spreading around the middle like he was. The only other difference was that she wore a smooth leather jacket, with a tarnished and dented aluminium case hanging on a worn strap from her shoulder.

"Tell me, why are you called Zozo?" Ian asked after they had looked at each other silently for a few moments.

"Because I work in what we call in French 'la zone'," she replied. "That means anything from featureless industrial estates to dangerous places like Bidonsol. We French like to chop names up, and we like alliteration. My real name is Nadine Berthaud, but everyone except my mother calls me Zozo. I'm completely used to it now."

"Do you mind if I call you Zozo?"

"No."

"Tell me how you unlocked my door, and how did you check the hotel reservation system?"

"That is part of the trade of networking exploring. Perhaps I am what you call a poacher turned gamekeeper, or perhaps some of the habits of the people I track have rubbed off on to me. Opening this kind of electronic lock is easy, especially when you can talk to the hotel computer."

Suddenly she turned and walked over to the door and Ian started to panic. However she only pulled the safety catch into place. She turned back into the room and smiled to him.

"Now that I'm here, I might as well ensure you are safe until morning," she said with a smile that removed all his fears. "What do you wear to bed?"

"Nothing," Ian replied, startled.

"Good," Zozo said with a grin, "so do I."

And then she started to undress. Ian watched in fascination as the T-shirt came off to reveal pale brown skin, small breasts and that she did not shave under her arms. She wore tiny cotton briefs, but not for long. Her legs were smooth and firm, and she looked as if she kept herself fit. Ian was too moved to say anything, but reached out to take her hands.

"Zozo, you are so beautiful and fit. I am pale, and fat, and unfit. Can you like me?"

"Don't be silly. Of course I can. Don't worry."

"Zozo, I've been on my own for a few years ... I don't know what will ..."

"I tell you, don't worry. I've been on my own for a while now too. We both need to learn about each other. We're on two adventures now," Zozo said, "one for work, and one for us. In the best adventures you feel, you know that the outcome will be good, will be worth it, and it makes even the hardest roads seem worth following."

She freed one hand from his to pull the bed sheets back from him. "How could I not like you!" she said looking at him slowly. As she climbed in beside him he noticed how beautifully the darkness of her skin contrasted against his whiteness.

"Zozo..."

She put a finger over his mouth. "I tell you, don't worry. Don't say anything. In the morning we will talk, now we need to discover each other a little." Ian felt her hands exploring his body, and to his surprise, found his arms folding around her, pulling them together.

Once again Ian found himself wide-awake. Light was coming in around the curtain and he saw that it was 7.40. Zozo was asleep close beside him. She smelt wonderful. But above her regular breathing Ian heard a noise in the corridor again. All his fears of organised crime rushed back.

The door opened slightly and stuck with a bang on the safety catch. He heard a familiar nasal, female voice from outside. "Ian, have they done it again? It's Judith. I'll go and get another room. Sorry to disturb you." And the door closed again.

Ian collapsed back with a sigh into the pillows.

"Ian, who was that?" Zozo asked.

"A colleague from WIN in the US. Somehow, someone keeps booking us into the same hotel room. I hope it doesn't happen again, especially now that I have you."

"So you have me now?" Zozo asked with a grin.

"Zozo, no joke. I don't know if I have you, but I hope I do. No one has ever made such an impact on me. I just hope that I can persuade you to love me."

"We don't know each other enough to know if we love, yet." Zozo replied. "But, Ian, believe me I want to get to know you much, much better." And she paused. "And tonight I slept better than I have for a long, long time. Thank you."

"I know what you mean. I do feel better than for years." Ian said. "Shall we have breakfast and talk, or do you want to get to know me some more?"

While they laughed, the phone rang.

"Ian, it's Judith. I'm really very sorry for the disturbance. I must bring you up to date, that's why I came over so early. Can you meet me for breakfast?"

"Ok, but in half and hour. I'm still in bed." Ian replied, and hung up. He turned to Zozo and explained.

"Let's shower, and go meet this Judith."

Judith was waiting, primly dressed as usual in a high-necked floral dress. Ian and Zozo were wearing leggings and T-shirts: his bright, hers black. Judith looked surprised.

"Judith, please meet my new friend Zozo. Zozo, Judith, from Boston." Ian said. "Zozo is our network explorer for Paris. We seem to have struck up a close relationship, haven't we?" And they smiled brightly at each other.

"Oh. Well, it sounds like we're well set up then. Do you have any news?"

"I have located the machine's street address," Zozo replied as she sat down. "But it is not a safe place to go at night, and only slightly better by day. Ian will need some different clothes to go there." She paused. "I do not think, Judith, that you should come with us."

"Suits me fine, not my job." Judith replied. "I work in a different way from you techies. I look at corporate and people structures, and I have found something a bit alarming."

"Good," said Ian. "I like working with efficient people. Tell us about it."

"Ian asked me to find out how someone could enter a false fault report on a chiller." Judith explained to Zozo. "So I looked at the procedures. Turns out that the environmental systems were easy to access, but there was a record of who had entered the areas. I also checked back to see what fault reports had been entered. What I found was so alarming that I left London immediately. If someone finds out what I have been looking at then we are rumbled.

"I found that there were six faults logged over a period of three weeks, enough to raise a call to Permanent Network. For each of those faults there were matching entries into the area from the same member of the cleaning company.

"That may sound careless, but it wasn't. Each time there was a delay of six hours between entry and the fault log, so there must have been some kind of device to insert the fault. What was bad, or again lucky for us, was that it was not the normal cleaner in the area. He was on vacation, and there was a stand in."

"And don't tell me, he had joined the cleaning company a month before and left shortly after," Ian added.

"Correct," Judith continued. "But that was the easy part, and with Ashley's help I could cover up what I was doing. What scares me was that I found something unusual. All contractors have to have a check performed by a director-level manager. I looked to see who had cleared the cyberplumber you call Red, and the mystery cleaner. It was the same man, and these were the only people he had cleared. It just so happened that the person who would normally had given clearance had been on travel both of those days.

"Ashley was very worried, because she felt this was too obvious, and that there were probably some kind of traps round those entries. We look them up and alarm bells ring. We were careful to do the look ups with my ID to protect Ashley's location."

"But why are you so worried?" Ian asked.

"Because the person who authorised Red and the cleaner was an editorial director. His name is Hugo Blunt and he has direct responsibility for controlling crime-related coverage. Who better to be able to lean on if you're an organised criminal?"

"Oh dear. So it looks even more like crime." Ian said. "So what are you doing here? You're not exactly lying low. I appreciate the information and all that, but what can you do?"

"Mainly I'm here in Paris because it was where the first runner out of London was going. Secondly because you needed to know what I've just told you and we did not want to use mail or a call. And last, I have what I think is an important lead I need to follow up here."

"I wish someone would tell me some more," Zozo said, "Now I've heard of criminal involvement. Not that I mind, it's not the first time I've trailed wire for something that turned out to be less than sanitary. But I do like to know."

"Zozo, it seems Ian has been remiss in telling you what he is up to," Judith said, "or perhaps he had more pressing business with you? I take it you've spent the night together. When did you meet?"

"Yesterday, shortly after I arrived." Ian answered.

"Really, and you're already intimate. I can't understand that at all. My fiancé and I have been engaged for a year and we've known each other for two. We are only now considering intimate relations."

"So tell me, Judith," Zozo asked, "why are you engaged to this fiancé?"

"We met at a concert and we discovered a joint passion for the works of Elliot Carter," said Judith.

"I think we can say that Ian and I met at work and discovered a joint passion for each other. We both felt it. And it was me that came here, so don't blame poor naive Ian!" Zozo exclaimed, squeezing Ian's hand as his face turned red.

"Ian and Zozo, I wish you all the best, I do, but it's just I'm surprised at the speed." Judith said with sincerity. "I just hope we manage to achieve our mission for you both to live happily ever after. Now tell me what you two have found, other than each other."

"Remember Red? Her name is Tamzen Shapiro but goes by the name Rouge and she is a maverick hacker." Ian answered. "I've been tracing her and, frankly, failed. She seems to have disappeared from the scene here about six years ago, and no one knows where to. Her work is distinctive, and would have been seen by some of my friends. I had some espressos with old acquaintances last night - "

"Ian, you said you could not sleep for thinking of me, but it was too much coffee!" Zozo interrupted, then laughed out loud when she saw his face. "It's only a joke," and she planted a kiss on his cheek.

"- and they all seemed to have heard of her. She is brilliant, better even than me I fear. But strange, and with a warped system of values. One no one can understand, and some of my friends here in Hackville are quite unusual themselves. No one disappears. Everyone leaves at least an email address, or is spotted on the net, but not Rouge. Wherever she has gone, she is not on the internet under any of her names." Ian concluded.

"Oh, that is odd." Judith said. "And Zozo, I appreciate you are new to the party, but what news do you have?"

"I have traced the physical location of the machine at the Internet address Ian gave me. It must be approximately correct as I've sent standard network testing packets to it, and it is on the right trunk." Zozo said. "The next stage is to go in and find where the machine actually is. It may have moved, at least a little bit.

"The problem is that the recorded location is in a storage unit in Bidonsol. That is the underground levels of here, the former La Defense area. It has been taken over by some people seeking privacy to perform their business, or that is how they like to see it. The trades that have always liked to hide in the dark to make their customers pay more. It's all small stuff, petty criminals, exploitation.

"We do not need to fear organised crime in Bidonsol, or not much. Serious crime is done from smart downtown offices; it is only the small-time hoodlums, hookers, and traders in the unusual who seek out such places. And then a change comes. Bidonsol was once truly dangerous, but now it is almost like a tourist attraction. At least in the main streets, where there are security guards to stop the tourists being attacked, or seeing anything too violent. Protecting commercial interests you understand.

"But there are back areas, and that is where the machine seems to be. Behind the safety curtain of neon, beyond the painted blackness, into the dark parts." Zozo smiled brightly, squeezed Ian's hand again, and said, "It should be fun."

eight

After breakfast Judith set off for the city centre to follow up her idea. Zozo explained to Ian what they had to do for the rest of the day. First he needed different clothes for their adventure into Bidonsol to find the machine that sent the fake news items to London.

"If you go dressed like you normally do, people will think you're a tourist. If that happens we'll be followed everywhere by dealers." Zozo said. "We need to get away from them, away from the main streets into the back areas. If we go dressed in EuroBell overalls we'd attract thieves after our tools. You'll need some different stuff to wear and some kind of official ID. I've asked Jacques Dupuis to make you a contractor's badge like the one I have."

"So what do I have to dress like?" asked Ian.

"Oh, a bit dark and shabby. Something classic, in denim and leather. But worn looking." she answered. "We'll go to the Marché aux Puces now to look for them. And you'll need some kind of bag to carry your deck in, except it mustn't look as if it has a computer in it."

"Ok, so I have to try and look like some kind of thug with a bag of weapons?"

"Close enough!" Zozo answered laughing. "But first you must kiss me some more."

———————

A couple of hours later they were taking a cup of espresso in a small café beside the flea market and looking at their purchases. Ian had a pair of worn black jeans, about which he was very excited.

"Look!" he had cried, "these are genuine black Levis 501s! That was the classic hacker look of the eighties and nineties; just add a computer-company T-shirt and walking boots and that was it. And besides, 501s were the only cash cow in the fashion business; they made them for years and years, on and on making money without any changes."

Zozo patted him tolerantly on the back and said, "It looks like a pair of trousers to me!"

That morning Zozo had chosen a dark, plain T-shirt for Ian, and they had bought what she called a Perfecto: a leather jacket. The outfit was to be completed by a pair of boots, but Ian had refused to wear second-hand boots.

"Why do I need boots anyway?" he had asked.

"Because there is all sorts of debris in the dark areas, some of it sharp, some of it poisonous, and some of it alive." Zozo explained. "You have to be able to walk without looking down too much. You need at least your ankles covered."

"But even thugs must buy new shoes sometimes," Ian complained. "Can't I just go to a shop and get some nice, clean plain boots?"

He'd made a sad face and she had laughingly agreed. The bag for the computer, however, had come from the flea market. Ian was pleased to have found a plumber's bag much like the one Bruce had carried in London. It was made of old leather, creased and stained in a comfortable way. Someone had wrapped string round the handles like Ian's grandfather had done, but neither he nor his father had ever managed to do.

"Now that we have all your new clothes," Zozo said, after she finished her coffee, "we have to go and collect your pass from EuroBell, and I need some tools and equipment from my apartment. First I need to make a call, and maybe I'll cook you lunch at my place."

So saying she pulled her phone from her pocket and dialled a number from memory. After a short conversation in French with a great deal of slang she dropped the phone back in her pocket, looked up and said "Sorry, we'll have lunch in Bidonsol. That way I can get directions from Xian. He knows most of the back paths in there. He's one of the few people who actually live underground, and has been there for a long time. But at least you'll see where I live. Then we will have to go to EuroBell to get your badge."

"I'd love to visit your apartment, Zozo," said Ian. "But doesn't EuroBell need my picture to make an ID card?"

"They took it when you entered the building as part of the normal security procedure. All those images are stored away. It's just a matter of knowing where things are kept, of pulling out the right information and making the badge. We'll have to take the metro to where I live. It's in an old part of town and quite unusual."

They took the metro to Chateau Rouge and Ian was astonished to find that they emerged into a bustling African market. Small stands filled what had been, before the change, a busy road junction. Piles of strange fruit, sticky orange sweets, carpets and other exotica were on sale.

"This was an area of poor-quality, and hence cheap, housing in the middle of the last century," Zozo explained, "so many of the African immigrants moved here. Now it is a major centre of African and Arab culture. As you can see, business is booming. It helps to be on the tourist route too."

As she said this, she pointed to two overweight figures struggling towards the same road as them, pushing past enthusiastic merchants. As they entered the Rue Poulet, heading up towards the Sacre Coeur, they overheard the tourists complaining about having to do so much walking.

"It helps me feel less unfit and less overweight!" Ian explained, and yelped as Zozo pinched some of his spare flesh. However Ian too was soon out of breath as they climbed the steep hill and turned into the Ave Paul Gilbert, away from the steps up to the top of the hill. Like most of old Paris the streets were lined by tenement buildings, but strangely at the top of this one were three small houses built round a courtyard.

Zozo proudly pointed to the steel door, and said: "This is where I live!" She opened the door and lead Ian into the courtyard. A tiny fountain tinkled water into a stone basin in one corner, and some pieces of dilapidated cane furniture lay around. She turned to the right and opened the door into her house. The ground floor had been kitchen and living room, but had mainly been taken over by a mixture of pieces of computer and adventure sports equipment. It did not look like cooking took up much of Zozo's time.

"Wow, this is a wonderful collection of stuff!" Ian exclaimed, and gave Zozo a hug.

"Unfortunately we have no time to look at it now," Zozo said, "and our visit to my bedroom will, sadly, just be long enough to change clothes and collect one of my tool kits. Tomorrow maybe we can move out of the hotel and stay here; that way you can look at my toy collection. Or maybe not!"

Upstairs was her room, with a futon on the floor, some posters for ambient music concerts, and piles of clothes. In the past Ian had always ended up with tidy girls who had drawers for this, drawers for that. Zozo seemed to function like he did: a pile of things being worn but not dirty enough to need washing, a pile of stuff to be washed, and a few piles for things that had been washed but not put away. Ian rarely managed to get as far as putting stuff away in his drawers and hanging space. Neither, it seemed, did Zozo.

She was pulling off her clothes and changing into her Bidonsol clothes. Ian found this deliciously distracting to watch, and had to be prodded to put on his new clothes. He had not worn a pair of jeans for at least ten years and found them stiff and uncomfortable after his leggings.

As well as her bedroom and small bathroom, on the top floor of the house there was a large cupboard. It seemed to back on to the neighbouring houses. Zozo had to remove several serious looking locks from the metal-lined door and then she held his hand as the door opened. He drew breath. Inside was a beautifully set-up workshop and storeroom, full of shiny diagnostic and tracing equipment and other tools all snapped into place on the wall.

"I may be untidy with my clothes and not keep house like my grandmother wants me to," Zozo said, "but in my work I am pristine. I hear that your programs are beautiful to look at, clean and well structured. For me it is the tools and methods I use that must be of that standard.

"My mother was a manufacturing test and debug engineer for Dassaut, working with the designers to figure out why pre-production computer systems did not work. My father was one of those designers, however his thoughts were more on climbing and mountain biking than circuit and microcode design. As a result his designs needed a lot of test and debug, so they spent a lot of time together."

"That's cute," Ian said. "Where are they now?"

"My mother has retired and lives in a shared community in the Auvergne. She loves it. She looks after herself, eats with the other residents, and doesn't feel lonely. She does a lot of biking on the trails there. My father ... he fell when ice climbing in the Alps. They did not find him until the spring as he'd fallen through several metres of snow, then a layer of ice and again into deep snow."

Ian felt her handgrip tighten on his and saw tears welling up in her eyes. Ian was not sure whether to pull her to him and hold her until it passed, or whether she preferred her grief private. However she turned to him and pulled herself against him.

"Promets-moi de pas faire de bêtise, je t'aime trop déjà," she said almost inaudibly. Before Ian had a chance to ask what she had said she continued "But we'd better get moving." She held him tight an instant, then blew her nose, and snapped back into her work role. "We'll need some lights, locator tools, and the sesame kit."

"Sesame kit?" Ian asked, thinking of seeds.

"Yes, as in 'Open Sesame!'" Zozo replied laughing. "It is in two parts: one the bigger, electronic part, and then the smaller, mechanic tools. Actually there are three, the third one being very special and you're the first and only person to have seen it besides me. It is a set of ceramic tools for opening locks, small and slightly curved. They fit into a leather pack that fits in my briefs. That way no one can detect they are there: electronics do not pick up the ceramic, and a body search will not reveal it either."

"Where do you get these things from?" Ian asked.

"Did you know that to join the Swiss watchmakers' guild you did not just have to prove you could make watches, but you had first to make your own set of tools?" was Zozo's only reply.

At 2pm they left the metro at Pont de Neuilly, across the Seine from the old La Defense business area. It was an impressive sight, two massive tower blocks above the Míro fountain guarding the entrance to Hackville, and what had once been a busy road now lead down into Bidonsol.

As they walked over the bridge, each with their bag of tools, Zozo explained what they had to do to locate the machine.

"First we are going to have lunch," she said.

"Of course," Ian laughed, "this is France!"

"But of course," she replied with a fake accent on her normally perfect English, "we must eat before anything else. But seriously, we are going to ask my friend Xian some questions, and he works in a restaurant.

"He will, hopefully, have an idea of how to get the address I have. That will get us at least going in the right direction. Remember this used to be a mixture of roads, service access, delivery points, even a bus station. It was never intended to be an organised town, and if anyone does have a map, it is not published.

"You'll see Bidonsol Security people about on the main roads. Remember they are there to stop the tourists being attacked. We can't rely on them in the same way."

"I've been to Amsterdam," Ian replied, "It's the same in the Red Light District. A bizarre combination of major tourist attraction and vice centre."

"True, it's like that, except here there are dark back alleys," Zozo said.

They arrived at the first tunnel, which was clean enough and was gaudily decorated in bright, animated panels displaying the pleasures in store. Ian was amazed at how explicit some of the display panels were.

"Don't believe it," Zozo said, following his eyes, "it's just advertising. It's like all the shabby, sad places of the world. Glitter on the outside, pathetic customers, the exploited and the exploiters. The final product never lives up to the packaging."

"Sounds just like software! Anyway, I don't care for this stuff at all," Ian said. "I don't like spectator sports, and the same goes for sex. I'm into participation, and I'm into developing my skills on the same terrain, as it were."

"I'm glad to hear it," Zozo replied, "and I hope you're pleased to hear I agree entirely. I'd give you a big kiss if it was normal for two EuroBell staff to be snogging."

They walked on into the tunnel, and natural light rapidly faded away to be replaced by the glow of signs. The air was thick and unpleasant. Being a product of free enterprise, there was no central organisation that would maintain air conditioning in Bidonsol.

Although he had not seen anyone else approaching the entrance to Bidonsol, Ian noticed that the interior was quite full of people. Most of them looking like tourists, some of them rather obviously touts and pimps, with the security force clearly visible in their luminous jackets with "Securité" across their broad backs. Zozo had been right, dressed as they were no one bothered them. Ian saw a few other people wearing similar clothes and wondered what business they were in.

Ian looked at sex shops, strip clubs, and brothels. He noted with interest there was no discrimination: all tastes were catered for, hetero- or homosexual, male or female. He was also somewhat alarmed to see the amount of pornographic software, even a whole shop dedicated to it called Virtugasm.

"Who writes this stuff?" Ian wondered out loud.

"Not everyone is as pure and driven as you Ian," Zozo replied, "it's a logical extension of film, after all, and porn cinema has been around as long as cinema itself. They probably make a lot of money from it, and it makes sad people happy. I'd guess that there are techies and so-called artists, just like the videos, or computer games."

"I've never understood computer games, I've always preferred writing programs to playing games. When I close my eyes my head is so full of images and ideas that to put myself into someone else's artificial world is just not necessary. I'm maybe old, but I still like reading. When I read something I like, the words explode into pictures much more convincingly than any screen rendering."

"Had it occurred to you, Ian, that you spend too much time thinking, and that you're just plain lucky? Assuming you consider great intelligence lucky." Zozo looked at him seriously. "I count myself lucky to be able to switch off from time to time. Will I lose that with you, or can I teach you to skip some cycles? I love you Ian."

"I love you too, Zozo," Ian replied touching her cheek, "more than I thought possible in such a short time. I hope that I can learn to be with you, and sometimes escape from myself."

"How about lunch then," she replied after looking him in the eye for a moment. "We've arrived.

nine

Between the strip clubs, brothels and sex shops there were other merchants and a smattering of restaurants and bars. Zozo had stopped in front of one of these, called *Le Tam Pam*, which was designed to look like a 1950s American diner. Ian had been expecting a Chinese restaurant and had imagined some kind of noodle shack, however Xian turned out to be big, black and American. He was evidently delighted to see Zozo, and leaned over the counter to exchange cheek kisses. Zozo explained why they were there in rapid French.

Xian turned to Ian with a warm smile, extended his hand, and said: "Welcome to my diner, Ian. Zozo has explained that you are both on two secret missions, one for work as usual and one more personal. I'm very pleased to meet you and wish you both luck on both counts."

"Thanks," said Ian, "did Zozo tell you I'm always hungry?"

"No, but you've come to the right place," Xian grinned in reply. "May I suggest you look at my menu while Zozo and I discuss your planned walk?"

Zozo and Xian were soon engrossed in discussions around a napkin map of Bidonsol. Ian looked at the menu and was treated to an amazing collection of authentic American cooking, such as he had only seen in a California backwater while mountain biking with Marc. He choose a hot sandwich, a hoagie, and a seltzer, and waited until the route planning had stopped.

"OK, we think we've found where to go," Zozo finally said. "Have you chosen? I always have blueberry pancakes and a side order of home fries, doesn't matter that it's not breakfast. Down here it's always night time."

After eating they continued along the main route until they came to a shop selling various weapons that Ian felt should have been illegal next to a bar that singularly failed to advertise anything.

Looking carefully against the glare of the neon signs Zozo spotted a narrow opening between them, half full of litter. She pulled two caver's headlamps and a big torch from her bag. As Ian fitted his headlamp she motioned not to switch it on until they had left the main mall.

Ian had not really thought about it, but the shops and clubs were built out from the original walls, so the side alley initially led between wallboard and metal supports, with chaotic wiring running to fittings on the other side. From the bar they could hear the thud of loud music with sampled breathing rushing over it like waves. Eventually they reached the concrete walls supporting Hackville somewhere above their heads.

The light from the signs was dim now, but Ian was aware that they were in a larger space than the small alley, spreading out to the right. Ian also realised why he needed heavy boots, as the path was littered with all sorts of crunchy stuff, but it was too dark to see what it was. Zozo's hand stopped him and they stood dead still for a minute.

"Ça va", Zozo said. "I was listening and one of my gadgets was scanning for body heat. The path seems clear at least for the immediate area." She switched on her headlamp and the big torch. Ian looked down and saw a mixture of broken glass, syringes, and dermoblocks. This was set on a softer mush of dust and old food, the inevitable dropped pizza and spilt rice that had spoilt nightlife areas since the last century.

Zozo followed his gaze: "I told you you would need boots. This kind of dark corner is much favoured by the drug dealers. Although much of Bidonsol's money comes from selling drugs, the security people don't like seeing trade or consumption on the main mall. It upsets the tourists, so it comes in here, behind the shops. Now we have to find some other further back alleys. Stay close to me and don't touch anything OK?"

Ian looked up at the cable trays above his head and realised that power and data flowed down here in great amounts. Zozo and her colleagues must come down here quite often to tend to the networks, he thought. Pulling out the napkin map Zozo headed off quickly and quietly down the former service road.

A light showed ahead and Ian touched Zozo's arm and gave her a questioning look. "Its probably a back bar", she said. "Most of the people who work in Bidonsol live outside, but some people live down here. Xian does, for some reason of his own. Those people have made themselves comfortable in old service cupboards and the like, and as for other people, they need food, drink and company. However let's put out our lights until we pass it."

Ian had hoped to catch a glimpse of the denizens of this strange place, but his hopes were dashed as the bar, called *Le Zinc en Bois*, had a frosted glass door. Round the door there were clear tracks where crates were wheeled in and out, but they continued in the direction they were heading.

"There must be another way in and out down here," Zozo commented when they were safely back in the dark. "They bring in their supplies this way. Maybe there is a lift up to the surface. I'll have to find out."

Before lighting the torches she stood listening for a while and scanned for heat. All was again clear, so they headed on. Dark openings appeared on either side, some with dim lights in the distance, others half blocked with rubble.

"We're under the GAN tower here", Zozo said. "It used to belong to an insurance company. When The Change happened they lost most of their business as it was in cars. So they cleared out of their huge building pretty quickly. That was the first building the software people started to convert above, and the first that was taken over underground. Those lights are some houses and a couple of food shops. Did you see the trolley tracks? All the food and drink comes in by hand trolley here."

Ian noticed that there were many more doors on the side of the corridor, almost of all of them heavy steel with big locks. Occasionally big bunches of cables and fibres swung down from the rack on the roof and into the rooms. It reminded Ian of his visit under London, except dirty and frightening.

Zozo swung her torch to one side and found a narrow side tunnel. The beam settled on a number and she checked this against her map.

"This is it", she said. "We're somewhere down here. It's the best Xian could do. I'll scan it for heat, and then we'll just have to look for, at best, a code number on the door." She pointed one of her gadgets into the darkness, watched the results. "No signs of recent movement, it's all the same temperature."

Shining her torch into the narrow corridor she headed off over a thicker than usual layer of rubble. Not really knowing where she was going, Ian just followed, watching as she checked the occasional door in the wall. Usually this meant seeing if there were any cables running down from the roof duct. Ian noticed that under foot was now mainly builder's rubble and bits of cable. This was the domain of the maintenance crew, and away from habitation.

After checking many doors Zozo stopped in front of one particularly large and well armoured one with a large sign saying BIOHAZARD. She checked the nearly illegible serial number on the door, and then swung herself up on the locks to check the codes on the cables.

"This is it," she said. "It looks fun to get into. I think the biohazard sign is just to warn us off, but I've gloves and masks for us just in case."

"Fun?" Ian said. "It looks seriously well locked. How can you get through this stuff?"

"I have some special tools for this kind of thing," replied Zozo. "Really there are three locks on here, one that works from a set of finger prints, one that works on a swipe card, and an old-fashioned mechanical one. The last will probably be the hardest since it is the least amenable to stealth techniques."

From her bag she pulled out a duster and cleaned the surface of one of the locks. When it was clear she produced a black box that fitted over the lock, and had just one button and two lights on it. She pressed the button and one light pulsed red.

"While that is working out how to open the door, we can put on gloves and masks," Zozo said.

"Wait," said Ian. "How can that open a print lock?"

"Easy!" said Zozo. "Inside the lock is a small computer, right? It's got a memory with the set of fingerprints that will trigger the lock, and a processor that compares the print on the outside with the one in memory. You're a software guy, you understand this stuff. So what my box does is try putting finger prints against the exterior plate and listens to the spurious radio emissions from the internal bus. From that it picks up details of what is accepted and slowly reconstructs a full authorised print image."

"Shit, it's as easy as that?"

"Nobody said it was easy! There is a lot of work in that process, and some old spy techniques involved. Most people gave up voice recognition security a long time ago as it was too easy to crack this way. Believe it or not the hardest part is building something electronic that the detector plate will accept. Guess how that was cracked?"

"More military stuff?" Ian hazarded.

"No - from the people who make the locks themselves. They have to test that the locks work before they ship them, OK? So it's too expensive to have real people testing each lock, so they devised a testing machine that could trigger the lock's sensitive panel. The crackers just took one of those and built the smarts on the back to understand what the lock was up to. And do you know who the crackers are?"

"The military?" Ian tried again.

"Wrong again. It's the lock makers themselves. They had a few problems with rich elderly customers who locked their papers in print-secured safes, and then died. Since the deceased person had only saved one set of prints in the lock the family could not open it. Breaking into safes is very difficult and messy, especially since they only use print locks on expensive ones. So the makers made a small number of devices for opening the locks and did not tell many people about them. In the world of cyberplumbers it's a trade secret that they exist."

Before Ian could think of anything to say the device stopped flashing its red light and showed green. There was a rumble of servomotors pulling heavy bolts back behind the door. Zozo tried the handle, but the other locks were still engaged.

Zozo planted a kiss on Ian, and gave him a pair of surgical gloves and a mask to put on. Another gadget like the first one slipped into the card reader slot and blinked red for a few seconds before showing a green light. While it had been working Zozo had produced a small pack of lock picks from the sesame bag. A few minutes of fiddling and the last, mechanical lock clicked open.

"Smart people," she said. "Three locks of different technologies is ideal. A lot of work and equipment to open them, and any more than three weakens the doorframe too much. Stand behind me. Since you've got your mask and gloves on, I'm going to stay behind the door, but once it's open, you're going to look into the room and see what's there."

The door scraped open slowly, pushing the rubble out of the way. When the door was fully open a spray of chemical splattered against the opposite wall. It smelt of ammonia.

"That," Zozo declared, "was the biohazard. A nice little booby trap. It's no fun being in the darkest end of Bidonsol with your eyes out. Carefully check the room now."

Ian gingerly peered round the door to see a surprisingly large and well-lit room. Inside it was a similar set of equipment to that he had seen in London. This time the computer was linked to a rack of what looked like radio equipment, except that it was labelled in some language Ian could not read. He looked around, and could see no hazards other than the bleach spray.

"It's OK, come in. There's nothing except a computer and some foreign radio gear. I'm going to plug my deck in and see what I can find on the local machine. Can you check out the radio stuff?"

"Sure, and take off the mask so I can kiss you again!" Zozo replied. "Then I'm going to remove that bleach spray as a favour to any other people coming in here. After that I'm going to heat scan the corridor again, *then* I'll check the radio."

"I see why you call yourself a network explorer," Ian replied. "There's a great deal more to your work than engineering!"

Ian plugged his deck into the computer and was not surprised to discover that it was called Rouge. He quickly confirmed that it was the right machine, and that it had some special device drivers loaded that seemed to be for talking to the radio gear. He had just worked out that it must be a satellite link when Zozo spoke to him.

"It's a satellite system of some kind." she said. "There's a couple of fibres heading upwards, nicely labelled. I'll bet these link to the roof of the GAN tower. I can check that out."

"That checks out with the software. What seems to happen is that our friends send the fake message to this machine by satellite, and this one forwards it on to a machine in London via the Internet. The machine in London then sneaks it into the WIN building and on into the network." Ian summarised. "It appears that there has been no activity since the message that escaped onto the feed. I wonder how they know it all works?"

"Can you tell what satellite it is talking to from the software?" asked Zozo.

"No, it just talks directly to the radio system. As far as the computer is concerned it could be a telephone line, a fibre, anything."

"That could be a problem then, working out where the messages are coming from." Zozo said. "Merde alors, we could be at a dead end. Perhaps I can get the inclination of the satellite from the dish and find out more from the comms database back at EuroBell. But it will still be almost impossible to work out where the messages are coming from."

"Shit." Ian said looking crestfallen. "We've been lucky so far. Now we may have to pass this on to the professionals. I'll just take some of the old messages off onto my deck..."

"Your luck has run out then," said a rough voice. "And you don't take anything."

Ian turned round on his chair to look for the first time at a Bidonsol tunnel dweller. Pale skin underneath a scraggy beard and long hair, a menacing glint in his eyes. Grubby jeans and a long coat, from which projected the end of an old rifle. His other hand was raised with a sharp knife pointing at Ian.

"We're from EuroBell..." Zozo started.

"Maybe, but you've no right to take stuff, and this *salaud* wants to do just that. You're going to come with me to explain what you're up to in front of the Bidonsol militia." said the intruder. "Pack up your stuff and close up. I've got a shot gun here, so I can't miss, and it makes a mess."

Ian and Zozo looked at each other nervously and complied. Ian had been able to down load the data he needed to his deck anyway. Zozo put her tools away, and stared hard at the satellite system, memorising some of the settings. Finally she pulled the door shut and flipped the locks back into place.

"You must be good at breaking into places," their guard commented. "maybe the city police would like to meet you too. Now walk."

They trudged back along the corridor the way they had come earlier, glancing at each other from time to time. Ian was white with fear as he had never been in anything like this before. Zozo looked more resigned than anything, as if she had had brushes with people like this in the past.

"We are real, we've got ID," she said.

"Don't care. He said he was going to take stuff from that machine. That's theft. We don't live like that down here. We're honourable people, we live by a code, and we don't like people from the city coming here with their loose ways" replied the voice from behind. "Turn right at the end of..."

"These are friends of mine," said a deep familiar voice. "What do you think you are doing?"

There was a noise of metal on concrete and Ian and Zozo spun round to find their would-be militia man held off the ground by a large, black figure. The shotgun lay on the ground. Xian had been waiting for them in the dark.

"I saw this creep follow you from the bar," Xian said. "I left Forrest looking after the counter and followed him. Did he give you his militia shit, no theft and all that?"

"Yes," replied Zozo.

"It's all lies; this bastard steals tools and information, anything in fact. He must have seen your bags and figured you were both a cut above the average maint'man, and so probably had better tools." Xian explained, shaking the man, who now looked small and pathetic. "He lives down here, near me. He has watched TV continually for most of his life. I think his parents ran old cop films for him when he was a toddler. I don't think he can tell real life from movies. But that is not an excuse. Now you two clear out of here before you get into any more trouble and I'll sort him out. Go back to the Tam Pam and Forrest will help you."

ten

As Ian and Zozo walked back from the dark tunnel to the main mall of Bidonsol, Ian slid deeper and deeper into shock. Zozo took his bag, and put her arm around him. She was alarmed to find he was shaking. Slowly they made it back to *Le Tam Pam* and she pushed him into a dark booth. Ian's face had turned white and he was shaking violently. Zozo put her arms round him as a tear rolled down his cheek.

Forrest, an old man with a world-weary expression, brought them two mugs of malted milk without needing to be asked. He gently touched Ian's forehead, smiled at Zozo and left them alone. Eventually Ian's breathing returned to normal and he drank the warm milk.

"I'm sorry," he started, "but I've never been so scared in my life. I didn't know what to do. We've lost the trail. We've come to the end of where I can be useful. I can't work in the field like this, Ashley talked about my boy-scout enthusiasm, she's right. I'm not a hero..."

"Calme-toi, mon pauvre innocent," Zozo said as Ian started to shiver again as tears welled up in his eyes. "If you're not scared shitless the first time you're in real danger then you've no feelings, no emotion, you're dead. I learned about this with a master explorer. He taught me about many things, including what to do when you're in physical danger like that. I'm sorry, it's my fault. I took you in there without any thought about what could happen to you."

"I've done what I can, I need to rest," Ian replied. "I want to go home, but I want to stay with you."

"Good, as I want to stay with you too," smiled Zozo. "We'll go back to my house until you feel better, and I'll call Judith to get the professionals involved. You've done a huge amount already..."

Ian's phone rang. He shuddered, and turned away, hiding his face. Zozo answered for him; it was Judith.

"Hi Zozo," she said. "I've some very important news, and I may have been a bit indiscreet. Can you both meet me in the hotel coffee shop as soon as possible?"

"Hi Judith," Zozo replied, "Ian's not well, can't it wait?"

"Oh, unfortunately not. I think we may be in danger."

"That's not what we need just now, we've just escaped from an attack. But I suppose we'd better come and find out what's happening. We're in Bidonsol now, so we'll just have to walk, slowly, up to meet you."

"OK, I can wait. It's a very public place here, so I feel safer."

"It's that dangerous? Be warned that we are dressed for work, which makes us look a bit rough. Our normal clothes are at my house, a long way away."

"No problem, but be careful how you get here," Judith said, and hung up.

Zozo turned to Ian: "Allez, mon petit brave. We've got to go. Judith has found something important and may have put us in danger. We'll drink some more milk, have a quiet cuddle, and walk on up."

Forty minutes later, they walked from the late evening sun into the hotel lobby. The security guards looked at them in concern, but Zozo flashed their room key and the guards smiled conspiratorially. They were used to people making sneak visits to Bidonsol while on serious business in Hackville.

Judith had not been exaggerating when she said she was in a public place. As soon as they walked into the coffee shop they saw her. She saw them too, but her smile soon changed to a look of worry when she saw Ian's still white face.

"What happened to you?" she asked.

"A nutter tried to steal our stuff," Zozo explained matter-of-factly. "A friend of mine rescued us, but it was quite tense. Ian's still slightly in shock."

"Getting out from Bidonsol into the fresh air has helped," Ian said. "I've never been in any kind of danger like that before, and I was frankly terrified. I'm at the end of what I can usefully do, as we've traced the machine and from where the messages are coming."

"Tell me!" exclaimed Judith.

"From a satellite," Zozo explained. "If things are accelerating, I'd better go and trace the dish and see if we can find out which satellite." She kissed Ian and left before they could say anything.

"Yes," Ian continued, "messages are sent to the machine in Bidonsol by satellite. The machine there sends them by Internet to London. And of course the reverse when needed. Zozo wants to use the dish declination and stuff to figure out which satellite, but I think that is almost impossible."

"I think I may be able to help," Judith said. "Remember I said I had a plan? It may be coming to fruition sooner than expected. I'm a process, social and people engineer, right? So I tried to think of other ways of finding who was sending the messages out and came to one conclusion. They must have some means of checking that their system works, some kind of test plan.

"The only way they can test the insertion of news items is to be able to listen to the news feed. The radio and TV programs are not enough as you said they were running short-life stories to avoid hitting the ship lists. So it must be a commercial news customer. So I cross-referenced the full news feed customers and the on-line information on the companies for anyone that looked suspicious. It turned out to be quite easy: one of them, Global Asset Control S.A., did not list any of its activities.

"I further checked and all but one customer had set up a filter to reject news items that had very short lives. That one customer was Global Asset Control. See how much work they put in place to make it hard to trace the messages, and didn't put any thought into the process? That is so typical!

"Today I went to the registered address for Global Asset Control, and found that it was a very small office indeed, but one with lots of computer and communications equipment. I said I was from WIN checking on customer satisfaction levels for news feed users, but I don't think they believed me. I may have made a big mistake"

"Judith, I'm impressed," Ian said. "And I'm even more convinced we need to hand the whole affair over to the police or whoever. Shiguru will know. I've found one of my limits today. From the sound of it you have too. I want to live."

"A noble aim, and one shared by us all." said an unknown voice. Two men had sat down at their table. The one that spoke was dressed in a conservative but expensive suit, had a pleasant smile and an easy, relaxed manner. He was obviously someone who was used to being in command.

The other man had the blank expression of someone who was only half listening polite attention. His eyes were hidden behind thick, black glasses. Despite not seeing the eyes Ian was sure they were continually checking the rest of the room, as if looking for danger. His hair was cropped short except beside his left ear where a thick plait hung down to the collar of his olive-green jacket. The same ear was pierced several times with some exotic-looking rings hanging from it. Ian wondered if the plait hid some cable and the ear rings could easily have contained contact speakers and microphones. The security man's classic zipped jacket probably hid hidden communications devices,

"Ms Planter-Smail paid us a visit today to check on our level of customer satisfaction," he continued. "Or so she said. And you, Mr McAllister, were visiting Bidonsol pretending to be from EuroBell with one of their network explorers. Oh, I am so sorry, it's Miss Planter-Smail and Dr McAllister that you prefer. We do like to be correct."

Ian and Judith said nothing, ignoring the jibe. Judith's lips were getting narrower and narrower, Ian noticed, as she tried to control her anger and fear.

"We at Global Asset Control are very happy to learn that WIN is so concerned about customer satisfaction and network integrity that it sends out such highly qualified people as yourselves to check on it. In fact we are so happy that we'd like to extend a welcome to you at our data centre."

"I'm sorry," said Judith, "but we're not allowed to visit customer data-secure sites without clearing it first without management."

"Don't give me any shit," said the man, losing none of his friendly demeanour. "You know perfectly well that my welcome, although most sincere, is not optional. Let us not make a scene in this nice hotel. We've already paid your bills and collected your bags for you. We like to make things convenient and operate smoothly."

"May I remind you that I'm a citizen of the United States..." started Judith, but did not get any farther. The second man had grabbed her hand and placed a dermablock on her wrist, a second later her body relaxed and her eyes went blank. She was awake but not herself.

"Now, Dr McAllister," the first man continued. "It's your turn. Again this is not an option." Ian's shock had started to return and he was shivering as the second man placed the dermablock on his wrist. All he managed to say was "Zozo" before succumbing to the drug.

––––––––––––

Ian woke. He was lying fully dressed on a bed looking up at a dull grey ceiling. He was aware of a dermablock on his wrist but had no idea where he was or how much time had passed since the brief interview with the man in the suit. All he knew was that he was hungry and thirsty.

His head was full of confusion from the drug, a whirl of strange memories. An echo from when he was very young, he could hear his father's modem in the room next to his bedroom repeatedly dialling an engaged number, trying to reach the Internet. Dimly he remembered the whistle and chirp as a line finally became free and the two modems connected. He remembered falling from his bicycle in the wet and the sensation of his head slowly hitting the cobbled street and bouncing in his helmet. He remembered being forced to swim in a dark pool and the terror that he felt.

Emerging slowly from the memories Ian heard breathing beside him, and he reached out to touch Zozo. Instead the other body spun round and delivered an agonising blow to his neck.

"Ian, oh my God, I'm sorry." said Judith. "I thought I was being raped. Oh I'm sorry. Did you think I was Zozo?"

"Yes," Ian replied with some difficulty, "in as much as I was thinking about anything." He tried to pull the empty dermablock off his wrist, before trying to sit up. Neither worked.

"I hit you on a pressure point, you won't be able to move for a few minutes," Judith explained. She got up and wandered over to the window, set in a dull grey wall. "We seem to be in some kind of barrack building in the middle of nowhere. There are a few other buildings and miles and miles of corn fields around us."

"Wonderful. Any sign of Zozo?"

"I've only just woken up too, you know. I can see what might be missile silos, and there is what looks like a helicopter pad. I've only seen them in films. Several satellite dishes and what I think are low-frequency antennae. There are no vehicles of any kind, no sentries and no fences. The buildings look old, dating back to the 1970s. All slabs of concrete and prefabricated metal window frames. I can't make out what the signs beside the doors say at this distance."

She crossed to the door and found it was locked. The room contained the bed, a metal desk painted olive green, a couple of metal chairs, and a small wastebasket. The only other piece of furniture was a battered metal wardrobe. Judith opened the doors to find it contained Ian's clothes bag, his computer in its plumber's bag, and one of her suitcases. She opened it up and examined the contents.

"Whoever did this has made a remarkably sensible selection of things I'd need, but no frills. Maybe I should hire them to do my packing."

"I'm glad you can find something to joke about," Ian replied, finally able to move his arm enough to rub his neck where Judith had hit him. "I can't say I find this at all amusing. Can you see any power sockets in the room?"

"Why?" Judith enquired. "Doesn't your deck run off a powerblock?"

"Yes it does, but the shape of a power socket is a good way of telling what country you are in. That or phone sockets, but I don't suppose there is one of those." He gingerly pulled himself off the bed, collected his computer from its bag and looked first at the date and then at the communications. "We seem to have been unconscious for eighteen hours, and we must be, as you say, in the middle of nowhere."

"How do you work that out?"

"Because there is no network coverage at all. The computer can't find any regular cellular, hotspot or satellite signals. That means we are somewhere desperately remote. I can't even think where we could be. No sockets, not even any fire instructions, nothing to indicate where we are." Ian said.

Suddenly he started looking carefully at the desk, looking for something. He pulled the drawer right out and looked underneath it. Eventually he gave up, looking puzzled. "This place is weird," he declared.

"Sure, but what are you looking for?" Judith enquired.

"You should have thought of this," Ian pointed out. "This is social engineering. In any kind of institution or big company everything has some kind of asset number stuck to it. Makes the bean counters feel like they know what is happening. That might have given a clue as to who was holding us or what country we are in at least. But either the sticker has been removed or there never was one," he paused. "I hope Zozo is OK."

"You've got it bad, haven't you? She'll be able to look after herself, better than either you or me, I suspect."

"You're right there, on both counts. She is so fit and never seems hungry. I wonder if they will bring us something to eat."

"And who are *they* anyway?" Judith replied.

eleven

Judith found a small sink and a toilet in a kind of cupboard at one end of the room, and proceeded to wash. Ian had expected her to complain about the cold water and rough soap, but she did not. Nor did she make a fuss about him looking away while she changed, relying on his natural politeness. Ian concluded that Judith had created her reputation for being difficult as part of her social engineering at WIN.

Ian splashed some water on his face, brushed his teeth, and lay down again. The combination of shock, drugs, displacement and hunger meant that he was having difficulty thinking. He found he was worrying mostly about Zozo, and not about his own predicament. It was easier.

Without warning the door opened and a woman wearing grey overalls came in and placed a tray of food and a carafe of water on the table, and left without speaking. There were two generous bowls of some rich, meaty soup, half a fresh, crusty loaf, a mixed salad and two cookies. A flask of strong bitter coffee made up the meal.

"In any case they are not starving us, nor could they be said to be treating us badly, I suppose," said Ian.

"Other than being locked up in some unknown location, you mean," Judith replied. "You're thinking about Zozo, aren't you. Funny, I've not once thought about my fiancé. Maybe you guys are right after all."

After that they ate quietly, each lost in their own thoughts and worries. Ian tried the coffee and declared it excellent. Judith tried some and declared it revolting, but that the cookies were good. They both laughed nervously, at which point another woman came in, and beckoned them to follow her. She led them along a corridor, down two flights of stairs into a basement, and along to an office where she left them.

A few seconds later the man who had abducted them from the hotel appeared accompanied by a young woman. Ian instantly recognised her hairstyle: it was Rouge, his nemesis.

"Welcome to our data centre and operations control unit," said the man. "My name is Lawrence Bolslovick, and I am director of Information Technology at Global Asset Control. This is my assistant, who likes to be called Rouge."

"What are you holding us here for?" Judith said. "I imagine you know that my father moves in government circles and there will be big trouble if you do not return my colleague and I to Paris immediately."

"Please don't imagine that we don't move in exalted circles too. Global Asset Control counts several senators and senior officials in the US as shareholders. And in Europe too, Dr McAllister." replied Lawrence Bolslovick smoothly.

"I'd like to go home too, but I'd also like to know who you are, what you are doing, and why." Ian said.

Rouge spoke for the first time, with a deep, assured voice. "You probably think of yourself as good, and of me as evil, Ian. Don't you? Let me tell you a little story. Leonardo da Vinci was probably the greatest designer, artist, engineer and polymath of all time. Imagine what he would have done with software?

"Well, he worked for the Borgia family, a nastier bunch of people would be hard to imagine. He created weapons and works of art alike. He led a good life and brought much good to the world, but his employers wrought havoc on themselves and all around. Have you heard of Benvenuto Cellini?

"There is an opera by Berlioz of that name." Ian answered.

"Well done," Rouge continued. "It is about the greatest silversmith who ever lived. He created the most beautiful items for the pope. The pope lived in many ways a pure and good life, but he employed a sadistic murderer and paedophile. He repeatedly pardoned Cellini for murder and child sexual abuse.

"So does it matter how you work in the end if all that counts is what you make? The good da Vinci built horrors for the evil, and the bad Cellini built wonders for the saintly. Is that us, or is that what you think?"

"Enough Rouge," said Bolslovick. "I don't think Dr McAllister is enjoying your game. And he does not know of what we speak. You discovered our little tributary to your great river of news; pollution flowing into the sea of purity. You figured we planted a network sleeper. You are right, we did. Unfortunately one of our more absent minded engineers forgot about such things as breakfast in other time zones, we are a little remote here, so you heard an item. We were unlucky that someone noticed.

"You have probably figured that we are planning to start dumping toxic waste into your river of news, to poison the world markets, destabilise economic balance, depose governments, and you are right. But only partly right. We are much more scientific than that. We don't want to create chaos, although we could, we just want to make money, lots of money, and help shift power into the hands of Global Asset Control's investors.

"We have a complete computer simulation for the major economic powers and markets. We've been streaming the news from WIN back here and correlating it with changes in the different world markets. We now have a knowledge base that can identify the kind of news to boost or kill any share you care to name. Our investors ask us to modify the state of a given market, and we can."

"If we were to simply flood WIN with false news," Rouge offered, "the banks would stop trusting WIN, and go back to checking more like they used to. Then they see that our messages are false before acting on them, so it is in our interests that we only let small amounts of misinformation flow."

"That's very clever," Ian said. "I hadn't thought of the measuring side of it."

"So it appeals to you," said Bolslovick. "It is not a weapon of mass destruction as you feared. We are surgical, precise. Would you like to join us?"

"Do I have any option?" Ian asked.

"No, not really. May I suggest that Rouge shows you round our facility while I speak to Miss Planter-Smail about her special skills?"

Bolslovick said, his tone once more indicating that this was not really an option. "Don't worry, you'll both meet back in your room very soon."

Late at night in his darkened office Shiguru spent some time trying to contact Ian. He tried the obvious methods of making a phone call to his deck, but ended up with the network provider's voice mail. He frowned, knowing that people like Ian never switch off their machines; at worst Shiguru should have been able to leave a message on Ian's computer. That meant that something was wrong with either the machine, Ian or both.

Next Shiguru tried calling Judith, who carried a telephone, but that too invited him to leave a message as the network could not locate the number in question. Even more worried he tried to raise Ashley, but although her machine was on she was not answering, so he left a message for her to call him as soon as possible. Although Shiguru had found a new friend in Paris he did not know who she was or how to contact her, and he did not feel it was worth disturbing Jacques Dupuis as more than likely she would be out of contact too.

After a quick check on who was in the building and a look at the street outside, he sat back and closed his eyes. After a few minutes he started to run a special program he had, accessing the computers that controlled the satellite and cellular connections than Ian's computer and Judith's phone used. If either of them came back into communications range Shiguru would be the first to know. Such a service was not normally available, but Shiguru had friends in the network company.

Next he set about sending mail messages to other friends, in interesting places. They were all security experts, like himself, all around the world. Soon his informal support network would be on standby. If any of his lost charges appeared he could get help to them immediately.

As Rouge led Ian out of the office and down a subterranean corridor there was a thunderous noise above their heads. In response to his enquiring look she said "It's the drone shuttle, a pilotless helicopter that links us to the nearest city for transport and material supplies. Although near and city are both relative. It's a long way to Androlovski, and it's not much of a place when you get there. As the helicopter flies there all you see are corn fields, and two collective farms, and that is four hundred kilometres."

"I see why there are no fences. There is nowhere to go. So where are we?" asked Ian.

"This is a former Soviet Union missile site. It was targeted at New York, I believe, but I could be wrong. Global Asset Control bought it from the local state army when they could no longer afford to maintain it. We removed the missiles and used the silos for secure data storage.

"One silo contains the archive system, and the other one contains the computation centre and offices. No light, but it's radiation and EMP proof. And better than your WIN basement which a humble cyberplumber can penetrate."

"With some help, though. We found who let you in." Ian countered.

"Really? Your Judith is really something. Different to you and me. I like your code, it's almost as good as mine." Rouge said smiling.

Ian almost said that he had seen hers and felt the same, but held back. He might need to hold on to that secret. Instead he diverted her off onto technical issues. Her conversations always had some hidden barb, as if she was always trying to prove her superiority. She showed him some of the machine rooms they had installed, and for his amusement some of the old Soviet computers they had found still running when they took over the base. Ian counted eight other people working in well-equipped offices on brand-new, high-spec computers. This was a well financed operation.

She took him back to his room after a couple of hours. As they talked Ian realised that Rouge had sustained psychological damage as a child. It was the only way he could explain why she was working here. Just as she was about to relock the door, she revealed it: "You remind me strongly of my elder brother."

Judith was already back in the room. "Hello," she said, "so you've been drafted onto the programming team?"

"Not quite," Ian replied, "but I have learnt a lot of useful information." He proceeded to tell Judith about their location, the drone, and how far they were from the nearest inhabited place. He was interrupted by a roar from the drone shuttle as it took off, swinging to gain height, and shot off in what was presumably the direction of Androlovski.

"So we can escape by calling up the helicopter shuttle then?" asked Judith.

"I suppose so, but we'd have to find out how to do it. And we'd have to be out of this rather well locked room." Ian replied. "If you can get me into a room that contains some kind of computer system that can call up the drone, then I'll call it up."

"Well, we're a team, that's for sure." Judith said. "You can work the machines, if we can get out of here I'll find out where the room is, and I know someone who can get us out of this one and into the locked room with the shuttle terminal."

"Who?"

"Zozo of course. I'm guessing the drone came back with her on board. And she is going to be looking for you, Ian. Give her some time for the dermablock to wear off and I think we can count on her finding us."

Judith was right. The shuttle had brought in Zozo, and she was put into a room down the corridor from Ian and Judith. The silent man had found her on top of the GAN tower as she checked through the forest of aerials and dishes looking for the end of the right fibre. When she woke she found a small, worried looking Russian looking at her. He was dressed like an academic; tweed jacket and corduroy trousers that were slightly too short. Underneath he wore a rough checked shirt.

"You're new, like the other two," he said.

"Where am I?" she asked. "And who are the other two?"

"You are in Global Asset Control's data centre, lost in the middle of Tchenchia. You must be a prisoner of some kind. The other two arrived yesterday, a man and a woman. The admin people here have no imagination, so they are probably somewhere on this corridor. Do you know them?" replied the man.

"I hope so, one of them is my friend." Zozo replied. "I'm called Zozo, what's your name and why are *you* a prisoner?"

"Uri Ablenko, Zozo", he replied. "I'm the reason you people are probably here. I forgot about time zones and sent out the news item that hit the UK breakfast radio broadcast list. So I've been put in here until they decide what to do with me. Rouge wanted that; she's dangerous. She probably wants me killed."

"Hi Uri," Zozo said, shaking his hand. "And what did you do here until she locked you up?"

"I'm from Moscow, where I was a world expert on economic simulation. I was offered a contract to build a huge knowledge base relating world news and economic performance. It was too good to be true, especially since I could choose my team and equipment without constraints. The only problem was being here, isolated in the middle of farmlands. It seemed like a small price at the time, as Moscow was very dangerous and the Russian economy was deeply unstable.

"That was ten years ago, and it was all exciting and new. We did it; we built a working model of the world economy. We can predict what will happen on the Tokyo market if there is a strike in a third-world sulphur quarry. What will happen to NYSE if the president has an affair. We have it.

"Then she arrived, Rouge. She was there to turn it all around, to make it bad, to take control. She brought two people with her to build a new system, to send messages back to the news network and see what they did, to check our model. I was pleased to see it backed up our predictions. Then she explained what they were really doing."

"Working out how to manipulate the markets according to their interests?" Zozo asked.

"Yes," Uri continued. "Just small changes here and there, moving small sums of money. But they have plans. I thought at first that they had plans to completely destabilise the world's economy, but no. It's worse than that; it's a commercial service for large, very rich investors. They want to be able to manipulate the finances of the planet."

"Who can afford that? We had thought it was organised crime that was running the show, the Triads, the Mafia." Zozo said.

"It is crime, and it is organised, and some of the Mafia are probably investors, but it is mainly a series of extremely rich and powerful families. I wanted to leave, but it is hard. Rouge knew I was unhappy and had me confined to the base for much of the time, and heavily watched when I did get away. And most of the team have been bought off with big promises."

"So why didn't you just leave?" Zozo asked.

"I said we are lost here, it's true. We are four hundred kilometres from the nearest habitation. That is a long walk and there are no roads. We see farmers driving huge machines twice a year: once to plant, and once to harvest. That's all."

"How did I get here then?"

"By robot helicopter. There is a satellite link to Androlovski Airport, which calls up a drone which flies here and back on command. It's kept locked and independent from the rest of the computers and networks to stop people calling it up all the time."

"Let's not wait too long then, sounds like we should be going," Zozo said happily, standing up.

"What do you mean?" Uri asked in surprise.

"I can do magic with locks, and my friend can do magic with computers." she replied.

twelve

Ian was sitting fiddling with his work deck trying to find some communications signals, and Judith was lost in contemplation. Another good lunch had been delivered and dispatched, and they half expected another visit from Rouge. So it was no surprise when someone rattled the lock a bit, and then flung the door open. With a yelp of delight Zozo flung herself on Ian, who was sitting on the bed, and proceeded to let him know just how much she had missed him.

Judith woke from her reverie and looked at Uri, who had been left standing in the door way. She stood up and walked over to him, eyes narrowed on him in distrust and surprise. Eventually she said "Since we can't rely on those two to introduce us, let me start. My name is Judith Planter-Smail. I'm an American citizen, and I'm a social engineer with the World Information Network."

"I'm delighted to meet you, Miss Planter-Smail. I am Uri Ablenko, one-time expert on economic simulation, now a prisoner of Global Asset Control."

"And he knows how to get us out of here!" Zozo shouted happily between kisses.

"Yes, that may be, but how can we trust him?" Judith said coldly, suddenly pulling her hand back. "In the mean time, Zozo, if you can leave Dr McAllister alone for a moment, can you get us out of here again if we shut the doors?"

"Let me check... yes." Zozo replied, closing the door. "Sorry if I was too noisy. Why should we not trust Uri? He's told me everything."

"How do you know it's true? This might be a trick, of some kind," Judith said. "I'm not sure. This place is so weird. I mean, why do they just not kill us now?"

"I may be able to answer your question, if you want to believe me," Uri offered. "You come from safe countries, where you don't have to worry about your government wanting you dead. I have grown up in Russia, where things are not so straightforward.

"Killing is a profession, it is not easy. No doubt Global Asset Control can bring in the relevant experts, but it takes time to get them here. In fact they are probably on the way here for me. I am now surplus to requirements."

"But that is not enough," Judith insisted. "They brought us here. That is a lot of time and money. Why bother? They could have found hit men in Paris. Hackville backs on to some of the worst housing in Europe. We could have disappeared in there any day."

"But all three of you are great experts, you have valuable skills," Uri answered. "Lawrence would no doubt like to convert you to his side. Most people can be bought by something. I was bought by the offer of huge computing power and, I thought, the chance to build the greatest economic simulator in the world. I fell in love with building a big system; that was enough for me. We're all here for some similar reason, and most regret it. Perhaps not Rouge."

"I've met Rouge," Ian told Zozo, "and what Uri says is true, at least about converting us. They made me a job offer. I know all about what they are doing, and I've heard the drone shuttle. Does Uri know where the control room is, and can you get into it?"

"Judging by the locks in this building, yes, I can open it." Zozo replied. "Uri says he knows roughly where it is, and I'm sure we can find it. If I can open the doors, do you think you can work the command and control system to bring the shuttle here?"

"Yes, unless it's all in Russian or something, but I'd guess that the drone is too recent for that. I wouldn't trust a 1980s Soviet pilotless helicopter. It's probably from an Israeli weapons company, and will be in English." Ian answered. "Judith?"

"Yes," she replied, vaguely.

"This is where you come in," Ian continued. "We need a good socially-engineered reason for us to be calling the shuttle. Something that the admin staff will believe if we meet them. Doesn't seem as if there is any security."

"No, there has never been a need for it before," Uri said, speaking to Ian for the first time. "And you could not have come at a better time, or a worse time for them, really."

"Why is that?" Ian asked.

"The first contract will be completed this week." Uri explained. "An agrochemicals company wants to change the balance of sales in Southern Italy. Substantially in their favour. That was why the message I sent out at the wrong time was about regional politics."

"So it was you?" Ian exclaimed. "How come you are a prisoner?"

"I'm a simulation expert," Uri explained sadly, "I did not want to have anything to do with changing the system we were simulating. But out here you have little choice when you are told to do something. So just like centuries of Russian rulers, great and small, they were nervous about me and were looking for an excuse to move me away from the software team. That excuse was, as I believe you guessed, that I forgot about time zones, and a false news item shipped at the wrong time.

"Rouge came to take me from my desk and lock me up. She enjoyed that so much, too much really. I was glad and terrified at the same time. I did not like working on polluting your news, and the risk of destabilising the world economy completely was always present. But I didn't want to think of what she would do to me."

"But now you can escape with us," Zozo added happily. "And help us unravel what was happening."

"But more importantly," Ian said, "stop the first contract completing. If they fail to deliver, the customer will get upset. Maybe even the investors will pull out."

"From here there is no way we can stop it," Uri said. "Even Zozo here could not get into the security zone -"

"I could if I had my tools, but they took them off me," Zozo interrupted. "I used my special, hidden set for the doors."

"- and we could not damage the aerials as they are too well protected." Uri concluded.

"Judith and Ashley told me not to do it, but I did it anyway." Ian said, turning pink in a mix of embarrassment and delight. "I changed Rouge's code in London. If we can get to somewhere where I can send an e-mail message, I can switch off the machine that feeds the signals into WIN."

"Or, if Uri is not what he says, we are now completely lost." Judith said.

"Mon héro," Zozo said, ignoring Judith. "In that case the problem is solved and once we're out of here there is no more worry."

"Not quite," Ian said. "Someone could restart the machine in London and the software would come back up again. Or someone could even reload an old copy. My trick is strictly temporary, but it does buy us some time to remove the link fully. It's an irritation for them, another glitch, nothing more."

"Well you could launch a denial of service attach on them with the off message," said Zozo. "That way you can at least be sure when they bring it up it will come straight down again. Sort of spam the machine to death."

"What?" Uri and Judith exclaimed together.

"Yes," Ian said. "It's an old networking trick meaning continuously bombard someone or a particular machine with e-mail."

"But spam is a kind of processed meat, isn't it?" asked Judith.

"Exactly," said Zozo, "but it is more complex than that. The reference is to an old television series called 'Monty Python's Flying Circus'. It's a bit hard for us to understand now, but there was a sketch which involved them saying 'spam' over and over again. Somehow that was picked up and used for this trick of sending lots and lots of e-mail."

"But they can still reload the old software, or Rouge could take out my changes, or even block my mail from arriving at the machine," Ian said. "We still have to physically disconnect their fibre from the WIN network in the long term. It's just that we've slightly more time to do it in."

"And there is another problem," Uri said. "Even if we can get the shuttle to Androlovski it isn't under cellular coverage. You'd have to get a plane or a train to somewhere else."

"A train?" asked Ian.

"Yes, an old fashioned, slow train," Uri said. "Tchenchia is still very rural, backwards, in many ways. Twenty years of small wars drain resources no end. No high-speed rail runners here; and most of the trains are mainly freight anyway."

"Well, I suppose we'd better get moving," said Judith. "We seem to have no choice but to trust Uri, and after all I don't see how things can get worse. Here is my plan. I'm a potential customer, or at least from a potential customer, and you are my technical experts. Uri is our translator for getting here. I've seen enough, I'm convinced, I'll buy."

"It is certainly very daring," Ian said. "Will they accept it?"

"Probably," Uri said, "the admin staff is entirely ignorant of what we do here. It could be a chemical weapons plant as far as they know or care. The engineering team would recognise me, but they don't come out much, especially with the first delivery coming near. We were running many large simulations of what would be the best way of disrupting the Southern Italy fertiliser rackets. It takes a lot of concerted manual effort to check that everything has been done right, the engineers will all be heads down in the silo."

"Let us take what we need, and get out of here then," Judith said.

———————————

Uri led the way over to the small admin block. It held kitchens, some bedrooms for the catering and service staff, and some other rooms that were sealed off with tape. Dinner was being prepared, and they could hear the usual kitchen noises as they tried to walk as quietly as possible. Their greatest risk, they had worked out, was of Rouge trying to visit them and finding them gone. However, since she was also working on the big simulations, it seemed unlikely she would be out and about.

The rooms were neatly labelled as to their functions. Uri read some of them. He looked at the ones with the tape around the doors and laughed.

"I always wondered how you could keep a group of soldiers entertained 400kms from the nearest town. Seems like the answer is here. These rooms are marked as 'Pleasure Chamber 1' and so on. So they had their own brothel out here. Amazing. But what makes me laugh is that after each room number it says 'No Emergency Exit'."

Zozo was scanning the inevitable overhead cable trays. "It's this one," she said.

Uri read the label, "Yes it is. It says 'Transport Command and Control'. How did you know?"

"It's my job," Zozo explained. "I can tell different cable types apart. That is the only fibre feed in the whole building and it comes in here. Luckily there are no smart locks on this door, just old military ones. We'd have been sunk if there had been cards or finger prints, or almost anything electronic, without my toolkit."

She discreetly pulled out the small pack of lock picks from inside her leggings and started on the door. It did not take long, and they all went quickly into the room and closed the door in case the kitchen staff saw them.

Inside was, as Ian had predicted, a modern console with only a few, clearly labelled options on it.

"You don't need me for this," Ian said. "You just have to push one button and it comes here. There are lots of other fancy options, but there are two big ones for ease of use. This system was designed for use in strange places by untrained staff, not for smart flying. So, do I call it?"

"Yes, of course!" they all chimed together.

Ian pressed an area on the console and a small display appeared on the wall. It showed the number of minutes and seconds until landing. It read 53.25.

"Good, that means that dinner won't be served until we're gone," said Judith. "That's one less risk of discovery to worry about."

"So do we wait here until we hear the roar?" Ian asked.

"No," Uri said. "There's a small cabin beside the pad. The noise of the drone landing may attract attention, so we want to be as close as possible. As soon as the doors are open, we run, punch the take-off button and prepare to get out of here."

They made it across the compound to the cabin without incident, much to everyone's relief, and sat down to wait for the helicopter to land.

"We are lucky that there has been no need for strict security here." Uri commented. "I have been working here on and off for ten years and no one ever managed to find a way of calling the shuttle. We used to try and work out schemes for amusement, and we found that the only connections were from the aerials to the command and control room. None of us had Zozo's special skills, so we could not open the door."

"Didn't you get lonely?" Judith asked.

"Yes, we all did. Most of us were young, male techies without much of a social life when we came here. Caricatures really. When at last we had a connection to the internet we thought it was for our benefit. But no, it was via the machine in Paris which was to be a conduit for fake news. I think Rouge put in the ability to send mail to the internet for herself; it was not part of the Global Asset Control requirements. She loves to upset people, including those she works for. She knows she's too good to loose. One day she will go too far."

"Tell me," Ian said. "You've lots of machines here. Where does the power come from?"

"Believe it or not, when the place was built the Soviets used to fly in oil to burn in a generator. Imagine flying fuel in every second day by helicopter from 400kms away! The waste, the inefficiency of it all. Global Asset Control replaced that with a biomass generator running on the cobs from the corn fields beside us. The collective farms process the corn and truck it to the rail head at Androlovski. The cobs are either turned into animal fodder or burnt for energy. That yellow container there holds the whole thing, and the mound you can see beyond it is what's left of the year's supply of cobs. Once a year a couple of huge trucks arrived and dumped the cobs. There is an automatic loading system, and the combustion is almost total."

"That's neat," Ian said. "And Judith, I had a question for you. What did Lawrence Bolslovick offer you as a job?"

Judith looked at Uri for a few moments before replying. "He wanted me to blackmail the investors. It is not that simple, of course, since his investors are very private people. He wanted to use my social abilities to look for cracks, ways past the armour. Chinks that would let him prise out yet more money.

"With my father's connections he thought I would be ideal. And good rewards, and of course, the constant threat of punishment if you stray. As Uri seems to have found out. I told him I would think about it, as we all have done. I'd like to proudly say that I told him 'Never!' and stormed out. But I didn't, and I am ashamed."

"Don't be ashamed. Of course you didn't say no. Only a fool would do that, it would mean no choice!" Uri rushed to her defence. "Much better to live on and look for ways out."

Zozo had been looking out the window of the cabin, pressing her ear occasionally to the glass, and checking against her watch. To other people it looked as if it had a uninformative designer face, but to Zozo it showed much more than the time. In the control room she had done something with it to set a countdown to the flight time. Now it was nearly over.

"I can hear the drone," she said. "So we'd better get ready."

"Wait for the door to open," Uri said. "Before then it is pointless and dangerous to go out. If we go out we'll catch the down draught and be visible from the main building. But as soon as the door starts to slide, we must all run."

Soon they could all hear it, and Ian picked up his work deck. It was vital for him to have it to send the mail message back to the machine in London, to shut it down. Nobody else had any baggage.

The black dot in the sky grew bigger and bigger, and suddenly the drone was dropping earthwards. Ian looked towards the main building and to his horror saw a figure. Even at that distance he could see the long red hair on one side: it was Rouge. She started to run towards them, but the drone was already on the ground.

The rotors blades started to spin down as the four escapees hit the pad, running towards the opening door. Uri threw himself in and found the take off button, punching it as the others piled through the door. Ian turned to look at Rouge as the door closed. The motor kicked in and the rotors started to spin back up, quickly as they had never had a chance to stop.

The shuttle lurched off the ground and Ian saw Rouge throw herself on the ground, covering her head with her arms. But he noticed that, even with the down draught, she had been smiling. A wild, excited smile.

thirteen

The automated safety message rang out in five languages as the shuttle helicopter left the ground. Ian watched the long side of Rouge's red hair streaming out in the down draught. A few other people had come out of the building to watch them leave, but nobody seemed to be alarmed or rushing around.

"There is nothing they can do," Uri said answering the unspoken question. "The only means of communicating with the airport is from the control room we saw, and only Lawrence and the other Global Asset Control leaders have access. They are all off-site this week. It didn't used to be like that; security has been increased over the last few months as we've worked on completing the contract."

"Will anyone meet us at the other end?" Zozo asked.

"If they do, we go back to my plan," Judith said. "I'm a customer and you're my techies come to check out what they are doing. That should be enough to worry anyone who works in aircraft maintenance. They won't be well enough informed to challenge it."

The former missile site was already disappearing in the middle of the huge corn fields. Only the mound of cobs waiting to be burnt and the aerials were still visible. Soon even they had vanished and all they could see was miles and miles of unbroken fields. The euphoria of escape had left them all tired and worried about what was going to happen next. They were free from Global Asset Control, for the moment at least, but were still in the middle of a former Soviet republic with no clear idea of what to do next.

"Well, so far so good," Judith said to Uri. "So far we can trust you."

Ian held Zozo's hand, and Uri and Judith soon fell into deep debate about something. They were leaning close to each other, Ian noticed. Judith had always maintained a large personal space in the time he had known her. Now she was almost touching Uri.

"So much for distrust. She will change her mind about 'becoming intimate'," Zozo whispered in Ian's ear. "You'll see. She's understood at last."

"It's amazing," Ian said, with a grin. "What a coincidence, finding yourself prisoner with a Russian software expert who likes the works of Elliot Carter!"

In the distance they could see the end of the corn fields, but they were replaced with arid, black soil.

"Why is the soil so dark?" asked Zozo.

"That's the tail from the chemical plant that the Soviets built in Androlovski. The pollution it caused downwind made the land sterile. What it did to the people we can only imagine."

"Is it still operating?" Judith said.

"No, it was closed down years ago. It was not economic to maintain it, being the main reason. The raw materials were shipped in here by train from Siberia, and the resulting chemicals were sent back to Russia the same way. No way could it be efficient. I suspect it was leaking heavy metals into the ground water too."

"What do the people do now?" Ian asked. "It's all very well worrying about the landscape, but people have to eat."

"Oh, a triumph of westernization," Uri replied. "With the expanding market for soft drinks in the former Soviet Union, they built a corn-syrup plant here to feed the bottling plants. That's why the railway is still active here. The collective farms deliver the corn directly to the syrup plant, the cobs provide the power, and the syrup is taken out in tankers on the train."

"Brilliant," Judith said. "A text-book example of how to rethink industry!"

"But there is better yet," Uri said. "Can you see the old refinery now?"

They all looked out of the windows and could make out the black form of some large works, with a small town beyond it.

"You see the points of light on? That's people working on it: welding, cutting. They are trying to create an industrial museum of the Soviet period. It is one of the few examples of this style of chemical works left, and it has all the classic problems. They are making it a mix of museum, mausoleum and theme park, on political and environmental issues."

"But who'll come and visit it, out here?" Ian asked.

"You'd be surprised. The airport and the hotels are good and have been improved for the corn syrup market. American executives come here and like their comforts. There are some that want to build on that and bring tourists."

They all looked out at the blackened earth, the small, concrete city in the distance, the miles of corn, and wondered. Not long after they saw the airport, and the multi-lingual messages started again, telling them to prepare for landing. They could see the small airport clearly now, and Ian saw that there was one, small aircraft parked before the terminal. As far as Ian could make out in the distance, people were loading baggage ready for departure.

"Where do you think that plane is going?" Ian asked.

"Don't know," Uri said. "I've not been here for a long time. But we can find out."

"We'll have to hurry," Ian said. "I can see them loading the bags."

The helicopter was losing height rapidly and taxiing above the blackened earth towards the airport. Ian looked down and saw that nothing was growing at all, and that the earth was crumbly and soft. He thought of that dust blowing out over the corn fields and being turned into sugar replacement with heavy-metal additives.

The shuttle was heading towards a small hangar that sat to one end of the airport, obviously its base, like a spindly mechanical homing pigeon returning to its loft. They were surprised to see two bulky men waiting beside the hangar. Beside each man was a metal flight case. The refuelling robot sat squat and heavy beside them, waiting to roll out and connect up.

"Shit," Uri shouted. "Remember I mentioned that killers could be coming for me? They probably came in on that plane, and that is them down there."

"No, surely not," Judith said with unusual compassion. "They are service engineers waiting for the shuttle to fix something."

Zozo looked at Judith in disbelief and just made a disparaging noise. Judith lowered her head slightly and said nothing.

With the soft touch of an automatic landing the shuttle landed perfectly centred on its landing pad. As the rotors span down and doors opened the two men walked over to meet them. Judith stepped out apparently oblivious to the heavies. As she turned round to talk to the three still waiting in the helicopter they took her arms.

"Take your hands off me, *now*." she yelled at the men. "I'm a Global Asset Control customer, and if you think I'll report favour -"

"Shut up," said one of the men.

"You're escaping," said the other.

"Damn right," Judith yelled. Ian could never really remember clearly what happened next. In one sudden movement Judith pulled herself up on her held arms, and kicked the two men hard. They dropped her and with quick blows she knocked out the two men. They fell to the runway with their faces just beginning to show surprise.

"Neat," said Zozo appreciatively.

"My father," Judith said between deep breaths, "made sure I learnt how to defend myself properly."

"Now let's stop this thing flying again. Any suggestions?" Zozo asked.

The refuelling robot was trying to work its way round the prone bodies towards the helicopter. "All we need to do is wreck the refueller," observed Ian, "and there won't be enough fuel to get back to the base."

The robot had decided it could not get past the two men lying on the tarmac, so Zozo was able to inspect it quite easily. After a few minutes she wandered over to the small hangar and came back with a long pole. "Let's just turn it over, and it won't be able to right itself."

"Like a turtle," Ian said. "But also like a turtle, someone else can turn it over." We should do something a bit more drastic. Can't we break the pipe, or pour some foreign fluid into the fuel?"

"More trouble," Uri said quietly, looking along the runway. In the distance there was another helicopter approaching.

"Ian," Judith yelled, "get your ass on that plane out of here, and leave us to sort out this mess. You're the bithead who knows what to do. It's more important to get you out of here to fix the net. If we all go then that will be noticeable. Grab one of these guys' coats and get over there."

"Yes," Zozo said, "we'll catch up with you. Believe me, I'm not letting you go."

Uri was removing the coat from the smaller of the two killers for Ian, while Zozo held him tight for an instant, kissing him hard before turning away. Ian squeezed her arm, pulled on the heavy black coat and reluctantly ran towards the terminal building.

Despite having been up late Shiguru was back in his control room before 6am the next morning. He had not slept much, but he was used to that. All the network traps were still in place, but empty.

Ashley had not called back either, although Shiguru had explicitly said to call no matter what time. He tried her number again, but was rewarded with her recorded message. It was most unlike her not to answer messages.

As Ian approached the plane he could see people boarding through the bridge, so there was no time to try to find a way round to check in. He had seen airline ground staff use the bridge fire exit as a way in and out, so breathing heavily he clanged up the metal steps, half expecting the door to be locked. To his relief it wasn't, and he found himself near the end of the queue of passengers waiting to board the flight.

As calmly as he could manage Ian walked back up the ramp and joined the end of the queue. The tired business travellers did not give him a second glance. As long as the flight was not full Ian would be able to make it on board, and out of Androlovski. Suddenly he realised he did not know where the flight was going, but that did not really matter. Where it was would be in communications range, and have onward connections to London.

He was glad Judith had suggested taking the coat, as all the other men on the plane seemed to be wearing the same thing. One more person in a heavy coat carrying a computer is less likely to be noticed and reported than someone wearing the leather jacket and worn jeans that Ian still had on from Bidonsol.

Approaching the door of the plane he adopted the nonchalant position of the frequent traveller who does not need help finding his seat. That way the cabin crew would not see he had no boarding pass. He smiled as much as possible to the attendant and was relieved to see that the plane had several empty rows. He settled into one as far back as possible and held his breath nervously as he waited to see if anyone else boarded.

Obviously Ian had boarded last, as the crew rapidly pulled the door of the plane shut and prepared for take-off. Out of the window Ian saw the helicopter land near the drone shuttle and shuddered. He felt a wave of panic sweep over him at the thought of leaving Zozo behind in the middle of nowhere, surrounded by enemy thugs. He closed his eyes and breathed deeply. After a moment he managed to concentrate on the flight announcements to see if he could work out where he was going.

———————

After Ian had gone, Zozo grabbed one of the thugs' flight cases. She found it surprisingly heavy, but being used to carrying tool kits, soon found a way to balance its weight.

"Now what do we do?" she asked, looking at Uri and Judith.

"I vote we try the old chemical works," Uri said. "It is quite near, there are no guards or fences, and there are lots of places we can hide. At this time of night the workers will all have left."

"Oh," Judith replied, "Would we not be better in the terminal building where there are more people?"

"Not here," Uri answered. "That was the last flight so there will be no one, and besides, the people here are used to turning a blind eye to strange events. The scars of Sovietism and civil war are still with them, even after all this time."

"Ok," said Zozo. "Wherever we go, let's move. Ian's vanished into the air bridge, so he should be ok. But that helicopter is getting real close. Judith, your clothes are too visible. Uri, drag off that other coat, and Judith, put it on."

Without waiting for a reply, Zozo started to walk quickly towards the chemical plant. The flight case was heavier than she had reckoned for running. She did not see that when Uri held the coat out for Judith, he held her shoulders just briefly. Equally briefly Judith touched one hand as it was on her arm.

fourteen

As Ian's plane lifted off into the dark sky, Zozo, Judith and Uri left the airport land and ran into the dark remains of the chemical plant. They were soon surrounded by rusty struts, tarnished pipework, and huge towers. Most of the valves, made of valuable brass had been removed, making the whole structure disjointed and fragile. A remains of what had once been safety notices were illegible and streaked with rust. Under foot the old concrete slabs had been stained black and sucked at their shoes with each step.

"What did they make here?" asked Zozo.

"I don't know," Uri replied, "but I'm sure it was toxic. Don't touch anything if you can avoid it."

After changing between lanes a few times and out of sight of the airport Uri stopped and looked back. No one was close enough to see them, but he felt sure that it would not take long for the Global Asset Control thugs to catch up with them.

Looking around them they saw a ladder heading upwards towards an instrument platform. They all had the same thought, and without discussion climbed half way up. He gestured to Zozo to pass the flight case to him. He too was surprised at the weight, and with some difficulty he hefted it up onto the deck with a load clang.

"We've just learnt something not to do," Judith commented dryly. "I hope the plane and the helicopter drowned that out." She paused to look up. "At least we should have a clear view in all directions from up there."

The deck turned out to be free from any noxious deposits. It was made out of solid metal with criss-cross marks stamped into it to make it less slippery. There were the remains of old instruments mounted on racks and trailing remains of an old wiring loom. Another ladder stretched upwards towards a catwalk that ran, drunkenly, between two distillation towers. At the level of the deck, there was a high lip made of the same metal all the way round.

Zozo imagined it had been put there to stop tools falling off and causing injury below. It was perfect for them to hide behind.

When all three of them were on the deck Zozo flipped back the catches on the flight case and exclaimed.

"Shit, these guys are serious."

"Why? What are these things," Judith asked.

"That is an AVM and this is a splat gun," Zozo said. Since the others looked blank she continued, putting on a tour-guide voice and nodding her head with each feature. "An AVM is a fly-by-wire anti-vehicle missile, this thing launches these small rockets here, and a fibre is trailed out behind it allowing the operator to steer the missile at anything, usually a tank, but could be a car, plane or person. The AVM can be used for surgical operations where less accurate weapons could cause significant collateral damage."

"And what is this?" asked Judith, laughing despite their dangerous position. She had picked up what looked like a plastic gun.

"That's the splat gun," Zozo answered. "It fires small pellets of poison. See these cartridges? The red ones are instant contact poison; the green just put you to sleep, like those dermablocks they used on us in Paris."

"What about the blue ones?" Judith continued.

"I hate to think, probably most unpleasant. The whole idea was invented to replace projectile weapons like rifles. You can't safely use them in planes, but these things can't puncture a plane, so they can be used against terrorists. And of course by terrorists too."

"And what is this?" Uri asked, picking up a small device.

"Looks like a talk-back set - it's a radio essentially," Zozo explained. "Put it in your ear and see if you can understand. It will switch on with the contact of your ear. First let me set it to receive only."

After Zozo had checked the settings she passed the small device to Uri, who put it in his ear as directed. "Yes," he confirmed after listened for a while, "I can hear what the people who came in on the second helicopter are saying. It's in Russian, so I can understand. Sounds likes they came all the way from Moscow, too."

"Another question, Zozo," Judith said, worriedly.

"Yes?"

"Why the rubber gloves?"

"Not for body fluid, if that is what you are thinking. It's so you can touch someone who has been hit by a splat pellet without getting affected yourself."

"Oh, we're in real trouble, aren't we? This is no game." Judith said, almost to herself.

Uri was listening intently, and Zozo lifted out the small missile launcher, clipped a charge into place and switched the device on. A small display came on, showed a diagnostic count down and then settled on 'Let's go, pardner' as its final status. Zozo grunted in disgust and put the thing down on the deck.

"They are entering the chemical plant," Uri reported, eyes distant and his face even more grey than usual as he listened to the Global Asset Control comms.

Judith was still turning the splat gun over and over in her hands, apparently fascinated by its form. Zozo gently took it from her hands, clipped in a green cartridge. She did something that caused a previously invisible panel to light up. A few fiddles with small controls later and she put the gun on the deck beside the AVM.

"What are you doing?" Judith asked.

"What do you mean?"

"With the guns."

"Oh, just getting ready to defend ourselves," Zozo replied. "I've set the splat gun to short-distance spray, that way we can't miss. You can control when the pellets break up into liquid, so that you can use them over different ranges."

"How do you know all this?"

"I'll tell you later. Now, get flat on the deck before they see us," Zozo instructed. "And whatever you do, don't get above the level of the rim. If one of them comes up the ladder, I'll zap him with the splat gun; it will put him out to sleep for at least twelve hours so we'll have no trouble from him. Uri?"

"Yes?" he replied, surfacing from listening to their pursuers. He had discovered that keeping alert and listening to comms was a skill that needs to be learnt.

"Get down on the deck, and keep you head down, tell as what they are doing if you can. And most importantly, can you tell how many people are following us?"

"So far I have heard three voices, and it sounds as if they are all following us."

"What about the ones I knocked out?" Judith asked.

"No mention of them," Uri replied. "They would still be unconscious, wouldn't they? I have heard no mention of them, anyway. I doubt if these people would waste much time on them."

They lay silently for a few minutes, listening for the Global Asset Control people moving below them. Eventually Uri said "They are getting near from what I can make out."

"Are they together?" Zozo asked.

"No, they are trying to approach the centre from the corners, but of course there are only three of them."

"Where are we, then?"

"Near the centre," Judith replied.

"Do you know what surveillance kit they are using?" Zozo asked.

"No, half of what they say is slang and the other half is abbreviations," Uri said apologetically, "it makes it hard for me to understand."

Uri's face went from grey to white and he breathed "They've seen the platform."

Then they all heard one of them approaching; slow careful, foot steps on the pavement below. Uri's breathing, already fast and shallow, accelerated, and what little colour his face had drained away. Years of suppressed anger against the people who had kept him a prisoner in his own laboratory turned leapt to his mind, and

110

as the adrenaline and hormones rushed into his blood, he leapt to his feet, pulling the AVM onto his shoulder.

Zozo, still flat on her stomach, tried to push him down again, but before she could, he pulled the launcher's sights to his eye. Letting out a dry scream of fear and hatred, he pressed on the fire button, without knowing where the enemy was, nor how to control the weapon.

———————

Ian managed to work out that his plane was heading for Vienna, which was at least in the right general direction. He also knew for sure that he would be able to communicate, to send the drop-dead message to the machine in London, and then catch the flight on to finish the job by completely disconnecting the extra fibre. He would also be able to contact Shiguru and ask for help.

The flight arrived safely late in the evening. He had tried to sleep, but each time he closed his eye Zozo's image filled his mind and he was racked with worry and guilt about having left her. He tried to convince himself that she could look after herself, and eventually managed to concentrate on what he had to do next.

When eventually the engines were shut down and the doors opened the sun had long ago set, and the airport was settling down for the quiet time before the early-morning flights started. Vienna had more flights than most cities as it was the gateway to the vast expanse that had once been the Soviet Union. Huge distances lay between cities and the rail network did not carry fast runners. Those who had urgent business still relied on aeroplanes, and reluctantly paid the high fares.

Ian decided that he should stay air-side of the airport to send the critical mail message. No one on his plane could know where he was from, and airport security would not let anyone pass through from land-side, so he was safe. He stretched his arms, which were cramped from holding the work deck, and walked off the plane, down the jetway and into the airport.

Apart from his flight there was not much activity, so Ian felt exposed. He decided he should hide, and hesitated before the first men's toilet. After second thoughts and a quick scan of the now-empty corridor, he ducked into the women's toilet, and locked himself into a cubicle. When he turned on his deck it immediately found a strong connection to the net and started downloading his waiting mail messages.

Apart from noting that Ashley had sent him something, Ian ignored the incoming messages. He looked through the information he had recovered from the machine in London to get its Internet address, and confirm the text that he had to send. With fingers stiff from nerves he slowly created the message, and sent it. He saw it disappear off the outgoing queue, and let his head fall back, eyes closed, and let out a deep sigh. There was no indication anything had happened, but he knew that he had done it.

Next he set to setting up the spamming loop on his machine. As long as his work deck was switched on and in reach of the cellular network it would saturate the machine in London with the shut down message. Even if they restarted the software it would instantly go down again because there would always be a shut down order waiting for it.

Global Asset Control could only send false messages into WIN now if they went directly down into the London sewers and reloaded an older version of the software without Ian's change. And of course they did not know that Ian had sabotaged the machine, so Rouge herself would probably have to go and diagnose the problem. She was stuck at the former missile base and could not get a flight to London before him. There was plenty of time for him to fly from Vienna to London and make sure that the fibre was permanently disconnected from the WIN switch before she could re-establish the supply of false news.

––––––––––––

Shortly after Ian's machine regained its connection to the communications network Shiguru's trap was activated. Snapped out of a light sleep by the alert, Shiguru immediately called Ian directly. The security man was shocked to see that Ian's face was stressed and tired almost beyond recognition.

"Where are you?" he asked.

"I'm hiding air-side in Vienna airport. Can you get some kind of guard to meet me at the door to International arrivals? We're in trouble."

"Sure, I'll arrange that and call you back. You can tell me what has been happening while we wait for your support to arrive."

Without waiting for an answer Shiguru hung up. Ian scanned through his mail before leaving the cubicle. There was nothing urgent, but Ashley's mail was rather strange. He had expected to her to be asking what the hell he was doing, or something like that. Instead it just said that for once she was trying to sort out something important in her life and for once the network would have to look after itself. She would be out of contact for a day or two. Despite all his other concerns, Ian frowned. This was most unlike Ashley, normally work came first.

A few minutes later Shiguru called back: "Your support will be waiting as requested at the International Arrivals door. It will take about thirty minutes for them to be in place; Vienna is a large city."

"How will I recognise them?"

"They will approach you and will tell you that they were sent by a friend. You must then ask who, and they will then say my name, but the names reversed. OK? Sorry to be so cloak-and-dagger, but it is the best I can do at the short notice. If anyone else approaches you, run fast and my support will join in."

"OK, but these people are ruthless, so running may not help."

"Remember that airports are public places and most concourses are under video surveillance. Only the desperate and the naive risk open violence there; our enemy is neither. They will try some other tactic. However tell me what has happened and where are the others?"

Ian explained in detail what had happened, ending with "Is there anything you can do to help them get out of there?"

"I fear that Tchenchia is out of even my reach. But we are looking at two very resourceful women: if they are still alive now they are probably safe." Shiguru stopped, seeing Ian's face and remember what he had heard about Zozo. "I am sure they have slipped they're pursuit and are on a train out of Androlovski. In any case I've set a trap on Judith's telephone -"

"I'll give you Zozo's too"

"- and when they come back into coverage I'll be speaking to them, and," Shiguru added, "to you."

"Good. How are we doing for time, as usual I don't have a watch on."

"Fine. I've just had a confirmation that your support is ready and active. Now go out and don't worry about the others: they will be doing fine.

fifteen

After speaking to Shigiru, Ian carefully opened the door of the cubicle and was relieved to find no one waiting. He washed his face in cold water and continued out through the airport, wondering what his support would be like.

As he reached the security door from air side to land side he stopped and looked at who was on the other side. A few people waiting for family and friends to come off the last flight of the day, a uniformed driver holding a name board. A typical airport scene late in the evening. Ian noticed a father with his two small children, all dressed up and holding a banner in some language he could not read, presumably waiting for their mother.

He noticed a girl with an incredible plunging neck line, the curve of her tanned breasts showing up beautifully against the matt black material of the dress. Although ankle length, the dress was split to the thigh. Her lips were painted bright red, and she was listening to something on small headphones. A small black box was sitting on her lap, and a slight amused smile curved her slightly-parted lips. Ian imagined she was dressed up to please her partner returning from some long trip. She made his thoughts turn to Zozo, and he wondered gloomily if she was still alive.

Ian decided it was safe to leave the security area, and walked up to the door. As it rolled back automatically before him the children looked up in expectation and he saw disappointment in their eyes when they realised he was not their mother. He could not help his gaze straying from their tired, sad little faces towards the girl's neck line. The warm expanse of skin and the smooth form of her breasts was very easy to look at.

Suddenly someone banged into him hard from behind, pushing his head down, and throwing him forwards onto the floor. His deck flew from his hands, skidded across the floor and smashed into a pillar. He slammed into the marble floor, hands up to protect his head but knocking out his breath.

Ian expected his assailant to grab his arms and twist them behind his back, as he had seen in many films, but no. Ian was surprised to see the girl with the neckline was up and running too, holding the black box tightly in one hand. The long dress flew behind her legs. He noticed in the clarity of a surprised instant that her legs were firm and muscled. His assailant too was fit, ran fast, and rapidly caught up with the girl, kicking one of her knees out so that she fell. Before she hit the ground the mysterious figure had slapped a dermablock on her neck. The anaesthetic took effect immediately and her body went limp in the arms of the runner.

Instead of immediately coming back towards Ian, however, the unknown figure picked up the black box and proceeded to hammer it repeatedly against the corner of a metal bench until it fell to pieces. By then Ian had pulled himself into a sitting position and, still breathing heavily, was checking to see if he had hurt himself or damaged his clothes.

He realised that the person who had knocked him over was also a girl, about twenty-five years old, and dressed in a one-piece smooth grey suit. She had a slightly Asiatic appearance, with short black hair. She wore an impressive pair of dark glasses with what looked like a rope to hold them in place attached, but which disappeared into a well-disguised socket on her jump suit. It was a very similar arrangement to the one worn by the Global Asset Control man in Paris.

Seeing that Ian was sitting up, his mysterious attacker grabbed the other girl's arm and dragged her over to where Ian was.

"Hi, you must be Ian McAllister," said his saviour-attacker. "A friend sent me."

Ian looked at her, dazed, and said nothing.

"A friend sent me," she repeated.

"Oh, yes. Which one?" Ian replied, coming to.

"Osawa Shiguru. My name is Minda. He asked me to come and meet you, mentioning you might be in some danger."

"Was I?" Ian asked.

"Very much so," replied Minda, "a blind hacker is at a considerable disadvantage. But let me explain all that later. First I want to get this garbage cleaned up." As she said that she pointed to the unconscious girl.

Minda pulled a phone out of a well concealed pocket, but before she could dial anything hostile-looking airport security staff had arrived. Before they could speak Minda started to talk to them in rapid German. Whatever Minda said was clearly effective as the security guards' angry looks were soon redirected to the unconscious girl.

While this conversation was going on Ian went over to check out his work deck and was dismayed to find that either the fall or slamming into the pillar had stopped something working. After a careful examination he discovered that the cover which held the replaceable powerblock in place was broken. The powerblock was loose and was falling away from its contacts to the board inside, removing power from the computer. By holding the cover hard in place the deck came back to life, but as soon as he removed his hand it stopped. He wondered if some duct tape would hold the cover in place, but even with his hand he could not make it work reliably for long enough to do anything useful.

Ian's work deck was effectively dead. This would normally have been an inconvenience, but now it was a disaster. The spamming loop had stopped, so all that someone from Global Asset Control needed to do was clear the incoming message queue, restart the software and they would again be able to pollute the WIN news supply. It was imperative that Ian made it to London as early as possible.

Minda had arranged for the girl to be taken away by the security men, but she had scooped up the bits of the black box. She took them and Ian to the small all-night coffee shop in the airport concourse. They took their place amongst the usual collection of tired and confused people waiting for their plane to depart or for family and friends to arrive.

Ian started to speak as they sat down, but Minda put up her hand for silence. She seemed to be looking carefully at all the people around her, but through her impossibly opaque glasses Ian had no idea of what she was really looking at. He suddenly realised he was still dressed in the Bidonsol clothes, topped with a Russian thug's coat, and that the pair of them must look very strange indeed.

Before saying anything Minda waved over the waiter and ordered two espressos. She turned her face to Ian, and let him speak.

"So what was the danger I was in?" Ian asked.

"See this black box?" Minda said, pointing to the bits on the table. "It's an optical gun."

"A what?"

"An optical gun. You may have never heard of them as they are against international law. It fires a light pulse of the right frequency and power to cause haemorrhaging of the retina, rendering the victim instantly and permanently blind. They were invented in the mid nineties, but the Red Cross succeeded in making them illegal. They did not like the idea of thousands of blinded soldiers being left on the world's battlefields.

"When the law was passed the military weapons people stopped making them, or at least publicly, and they went underground. As you can see it does not need much to make one. This model was doubly dangerous: the box included an image matcher. Someone had programmed your face into it, and all that the girl had to do was listen to it, confirm its opinion of who to aim for, and press a button."

"Was that what she was listening too?"

"Yes, and this box is really cool. It plays music too - see the soundblock here? It is designed for stake outs. All that is left for the operator to do is make sure that the victim is looking in the right direction."

"How did she do that?" Ian said, and then realised with a sheepish grin that he knew only too well.

"That was easy!" Minda laughed. "Attracting a man's attention is quite easy for a girl, you know, and she obviously had it down to a fine art. A very nasty art in this case. In the military days they used an equally unsubtle approach: they flashed a light to attract the attention of anyone looking, then blip, they're blind."

"That's horrific," Ian said. "Thank you very much indeed for saving me, although that sounds frankly inadequate. I had never heard of these weapons, and yes, my attention was easily attracted by her. Ashley, one of the people at WIN, calls it window shopping. Tell me, why did they just not kill me out right instead of trying to blind me?"

"If you kill someone outright in public it is usually pretty obvious who did it. There has to be a weapon and some kind of projectile. And it usually makes a noise. That way everyone knows who did it and the attacker can be identified."

"Of course, Shiguru said that the concourse was probably under video surveillance."

"It is. With a light pulse all that happens is someone is suddenly blind, and one person walks away. No evidence, and it could even be natural causes. Video can't pick up the light pulse, so the attacker cannot be identified afterwards."

"But surely the video will record all the people who leave the scene too?"

"Yes, but it would be a long time before the person suddenly blinded is able to communicate what has happened, then a long time before someone realises that it was not natural causes. And of course in any airport people are coming and going all the time. Remember that on video this gun is almost indistinguishable from a phone or musicbox. Looking at it from their point of view, I doubt if your attacker would have left the scene until after you had been taken away in the ambulance."

"Shit, you're right. Do you know who my attacker is?"

"Not yet, I did not recognise her, but then Vienna is a big city with a long and turbulent history. I could never know all the dangerous people here by heart, that is why I had the imaging glasses on."

"What do they do?" Ian asked.

"They compare the face of someone I'm looking at with a collection of faces. My suit has a cellular connection back to my office, and on via the Internet to different police databases. If it thinks it has found a match, it brings up the face, name and details superimposed on my view. And the glasses protect against light pulses."

"I figured they must do something like that as you were scanning the faces of everyone in the café. Am I right?"

"Yes, I must be getting too obvious."

"No, I'm just very observant, some say nosy. Tell me," Ian asked, "what do you do for a living?"

"Quality control," Minda replied. "Of people. Sometimes it's in expensive clubs where they want difficult people taken care of, like a high-class bouncer really. Sometimes I'm a body guard for important visitors, and then I control the quality of the people he or she meets. Quite often I work with famous people and have to make sure they are invisible, or keep the press away from them. We use a lot of sophisticated techniques these days to replace muscle, it's quite technical.

"I have to help you get safely from here to inside Shiguru's security zone in the WIN building in London. That means an overnight in a hotel and the first flight tomorrow."

"Well, I hope Zozo does not find out, I think she might be a trifle jealous if she finds I had another woman in my hotel room over night." Ian said.

"When I am working," Minda replied with a grin, "I am neither a man nor a woman. I'm a quality controller. Believe me, you'll be quite safe. If she's jealous that just shows how much she loves you! In any case, you could just not tell her."

"You know it's not as simple as that." Ian replied miserably. "I don't even know if she is alive or dead. I left her behind."

He suddenly felt tired and lonely. Despite having only known Zozo for such a short time he missed her, especially under stress. She brought calm to him, something which he had not known before. He hoped they would be together again soon.

Minda gently lifted Ian's head. "You had to leave; sometimes we have to do things we don't like, to do what we must. I'm sure she'll be all right, especially knowing you'll need looking after."

"When is the flight, and where is the hotel?"

"The first World Airways flight leaves at seven fifteen, and we'll be on it. The hotel is on the airport itself, but it is very nice. Don't worry, I'll look after everything, you just shower and try and sleep."

"'We'll' be on it?" Ian queried. "Are you coming with me?"

"Yes," Minda replied. "Shiguru says I've to accompany you every step of the way to the lobby of the WIN building and make sure nothing unexpected happens. You are far too naive to be out on your own. He'll look after you from there on. Now, off to bed. Tomorrow you have work to do. And I'm sure we'll be hearing from your friend too."

sixteen

As soon as Uri had started to grab the missile launcher and stand up, Judith had started to move towards him. The noise of the missile firing ripped through the silence of the disused plant. Zozo, gave up trying to knock Uri down, instead put her arm round Judith and held her flat against the deck, gently but with all her strength.

Uri stood, dazed by the noise of the launch, fumbled with the controls trying to steer the missile towards the enemy, except that he still could not see any of them. But they could see him. Alerted by his scream and the noise of the missile all three of the followers had located him, and as the noise of the launch still echoed around them, he was hit by a hail of poison pellets.

Pulling her head down further and putting all her weight on Judith, Zozo heard Uri's inert body collapse onto the deck. The AVM launcher clanged onto the metal floor beside him. Zozo risked a sideways glimpse, which confirmed that they had used red pellets: one of Uri's cheeks was stained red and his eyes were open, staring blankly skyward. The talk-back set had fallen from his ear and lay some distance away across the deck. Even if Zozo had felt it safe to let go of Judith she would not have been able to get it without exposing herself above the lip of the deck.

Judith was shaking violently, and Zozo had forgotten about the missile. When Uri was hit a twitch on his hand had sent the missile heading slightly upwards. In the split second all this had taken to happen Zozo had assumed that the uncontrolled missile had sailed out of the plant to land harmlessly in the dead soil beyond.

Suddenly a resounding, booming noise echoed round the steel work: the missile had hit and entered the tallest of the old distillation towers. Nothing happened, and she heard one of the hit men laugh, terrifyingly close to them. Then it happened.

Zozo and Judith had the impression that the air and sky disappeared, they could neither see nor breath. The missile had realised it had hit a target, and had waited for the operator to detonate it. After a short time a fail-safe mechanism cut in, and the missile decided to detonate, perhaps the operator had been killed, but that was no reason to abort the mission.

Since the chemical plant had been closed there had been no maintenance or cleaning, so the tower was full of chemical waste, soot, dust, and rust. The force of the explosion blew these out wherever it could, filling the whole refinery with dense, black dust, some of it burning. But that was nothing compared to the next wave.

Parts of the structure, already weakened by the removal of the valves for scrap, started to collapse around them. A huge cooling duct fell towards the deck where Zozo and Judith were lying, pressed one to the other, more for comfort than protection. The duct crushed the handrail, but stopped when it hit the lip, right above them, bending and flattening out slightly.

Other pipes and gantries started to fall away, removing support from the high tower. A collection of pipes and a service catwalk parted company from its mounting, and, bending slowly crashed into the duct covering Judith and Zozo, flattening it out over them, and pushing the gantry sideways on its pillars.

The explosion had weakened the already fragile, rust-eaten walls of the tower, and with all the surrounding pipework failing, the walls too now they gave way. Stage after stage of rusty distillation tower suddenly became a pile of loose plates, the edges torn and sharp. Lethal metal rain started to fall through the blackness of the dust, shredding everything in its way. Pipes were ripped open, cables flayed, more pipes and supports collapsed, and the concrete slabs broken into rubble. The noise of the collapsing tower was total, filling the blackness with a cacophony so complete no individual sound could be made out.

The air was so full of noise and dust that neither Zozo nor Judith knew what was happening, all they felt was the deck on which they were lying moving more and more, and being continuously hit. Protected by the cooling duct and the pipe assembly that had so nearly crushed them, they had escaped the mortal rain.

After what seemed like forever the noises died away to the occasional distance crash as something else collapsed. Zozo tried to move and discovered that the cooling duct was not flat, but covered in deep dents, making it almost impossible for her to move. The deck swayed slightly beneath her when she did manage to move. Judith was breathing but not moving; presumably she had fainted or was in severe shock.

Zozo began to see dimly as the dust turned back into air. First she could see the dim glow from the splat gun's indicators, then a rim of light from where the duct met the deck. Zozo had done a lot of caving when she had been little, before her father had died. It was not her favourite sport, but at least she was used to confined spaces.

By scrunching herself into a ball she could turn. After several cramped attempts she got her head near the edge and saw that the duct had been bent down almost to the deck in all but one place. There the flight case stood, strong and unbending, with the duct wrapped round it. Thick, black dust covered everything and choked the gap between the flattened pipe and deck.

At one point when she was turning she put her had in something liquid, and realised that it was the black dust mixed with blood. Uri's blood. She closed her eyes tight, spread her fingers wide and fought the waves of nausea that filled her. All her muscles screamed and her breath was deep and jerky, choked by the dust that covered everything. Images of her father flashed before her eyes and Zozo yelled.

It was a huge yell of anger and it echoed out of their cave and around the remains of the refinery. Zozo turned so her boots were touching the flight case and her legs bunched. She grabbed two large protrusions in the duct above her, pulled herself back and kicked. Cycling and climbing on the blocks at Fontainbleau had built her leg and arm muscles, and the box moved. Another kick and it was free, leaving a gap big enough to crawl through, out onto the deck.

Minda called the hotel and asked for the shuttle bus to come and collect them at the airport terminal. She explained she was travelling with a VIP, and required the bus to empty and named a driver. Satisfied with these arrangements, and after another scan of the few remaining people in the concourse they set off to the hotel.

Ian found he had already been checked in and all that Minda did was collect an electronic key and head for the lifts. Being a protected VIP certainly made hotels easier to deal with.

He had been allocated a room on the fifth floor. They stepped out of the lift and immediately he felt Minda's body stiffen. Without a word she ran away from the lift, dragging Ian, and pushed him into an alcove.

"There is a trap," she hissed. "There are recent foot prints heading towards the room, and there shouldn't be. They don't come from the lift or the near stairs. And besides something just feels wrong."

Again without warning she turned and pushed through a well hidden door at the back of the alcove, dragging Ian through with her. He blinked in the harsh fluorescent light of the service area after the dim night lighting of the main corridor.

"We've got to get down to the kitchen levels and into the security office," Minda breathed in Ian's ear. "I know the head of security here, and we can trust him. His office is safe. The rest of the hotel may not be. Vienna is a frontier town these days and strange things happen. That is why I work here. Beats handling rich kids who have nothing better to do than fry their brains with Flate, or worse. We'll have to call the lift and chance it, but we'll have to get out at an intermediate floor and run a bit."

"Shit, I'm too old and unfit for this."

"You'll survive. Now get behind me as I call the lift."

The lift arrived uneventfully and Minda called for level two, which was mainly meeting rooms and should be deserted at that time of night. From there were other service lifts into the kitchens and plenty of different stairs for escape.

They had appeared in a long, curved corridor behind the meeting rooms. The hard paint on the walls was shiny in the bright light. Numerous black marks and scoring showed where trolleys had been run into the wall as it bent round, obscuring the rooms in the distance. Suddenly the lights went off, to be replaced with glaring pools yellow under the emergency lights at intervals along the wall.

"Sloppy," Minda laughed, "we're one up on them."

"What d'you mean?"

"They have cut the power to the whole hotel to trap us in the lift, but we're out of it now. But that means they can work out which floor we are on, but at least they will try and find us first. We've won a few minutes reprieve."

"How do you know the power is off in the whole hotel, and not just the lights here?"

"The emergency lights, Ian. They don't come on for fun."

There was something about the way she smiled when saying 'fun' that scared Ian. He ran after her until they found an open door to a dark meeting room and skipped into it.

"I'm going to call for help, we can probably hide here until the hotel security neutralises your pursuers," Minda said. "Oh shit. I spoke too soon. What have you been up to? These guys must want you bad: they have a comms blanker running, I can't place a call. I'm going to do something I don't like. I'll have to leave you here and go for help. From what I've seen they will be hunting us with some kind of pellet gun, a poison spray if you like. My suit is pellet proof, and there is a complete hood and gloves hidden in it, so I can run from them if I need to. You would be knocked out, or dead more likely, immediately."

"So, I hide here in the dark, not moving?"

"Close enough. I'll be back with help very quickly. Now don't move or do anything foolish."

Minda moved silently to the main door of the meeting room, and slipped out into the public area of the hotel. A beam of light passed over the room as the door opened and closed, showing it set up for some morning meeting. When the light went, Ian could only see ghostly images of chairs before his eyes.

As Minda's absence stretched out longer and longer Ian's vision came back. Some light from the emergency lights in the service corridor shone under the door into his room, enabling him to seem more of his surroundings. In the centre of the room was a large polished-wood table. On the table was a projection system, protected by a clear plastic dust cover. On one wall was a large white board, complete with pens and a cleaning spray. Against another wall and beside the service door was a trolley loaded with cups, ready to serve coffee in the morning. Ian waited and worried.

Zozo clenched her fists and yelled "Yes!" to herself in exaltation when the flight case moved out of the way. Judith was still unconscious, so she would have to be dragged out of their temporary prison.

As Zozo started to curl up again to turn and grab Judith's ankles she felt the deck sway again, and saw to her horror a deluge of metal and dust filling her newly-created entrance. Clouds more black dust swirled around her, causing her to cough. Judith too started to cough, and that was enough to bring her round.

Like Zozo, the first thing Judith tried to do was sit up, and banged her head hard on the metal. It was very dark as night had now fallen completely. It was getting cold too.

"What has happened, where are we?" asked Judith hoarsely.

"We're alive," Zozo said, "but we're trapped under the pipe that save our lives. The missile brought down one of the big towers, and probably most of the rest of the refinery. This pipe protected us from the fall of debris - look how the shards of metal have dented it."

"The others?"

"I don't think anyone could have survived what happened."

"And Uri?"

"He was shot dead before the missile exploded."

"Oh." In the dark Zozo held Judith's hand. "And it was just starting. My eyes had been opened and now it has all gone dark."

"Yes, but it is night, things are always darker in the night time. And if we don't get out of here, it is not going to get light again," Zozo replied as encouragingly as she could, given the circumstances. Carefully wiping the hand that had touch the blood she reached over for Judith's other hand. With the movement the deck shifted again, but this time the gap between the pipe and the metal floor widened.

"That's it!" Zozo cried, "we keep rocking the base and we can slide out!"

Freeing one hand from Judith she swept up the splat gun and stuffed it in the top of her leggings. Taking back Judith's hand they started swinging back and forth, and soon the deck moved again, and again, each time the gap getting bigger.

Suddenly one leg of the platform gave way, catapulting Zozo and Judith and a pile of shrapnel across the devastated alley. The remains of the whole cooking duct and the pipe gantry that had been on top of it crashed to the ground, sending dust and rubble flying in all directions.

As the dust cleared Zozo made out lights in the distance. Suddenly she realised that she and Judith had been shouting at each other, having been deafened during the metal storm. She pointed at the lights coming towards the refinery, realising that the whole town would be on its way towards them. The dust and noise from the explosion must have covered the whole area.

"If we don't get out of here, we'll be taken to hospital, prison or both." Zozo said.

"And from there we won't be able to escape and we'll be killed by Global Asset Control."

"Yes, we need to find the station, and get out of here. I suppose I'm filthy with dust?"

"Covered from head to toe. We both must be. Not much of a disguise. So what is your plan?"

"It might mean a lot of walking, Judith, are you OK? You were unconscious for a long time," Zozo said. "This is the plan. The town is not that big, and we know there is a railway. If we just walk into town we will be seen and stopped, end of game. If we skirt round the fields outside of the town we will come to the railway. It won't be fenced or anything, and we can walk carefully along the track to the station. With this amount of dirt on us we will be practically invisible."

"OK so far, as long as we can stop for rests. I'm not as fit as you, and, well, this is not exactly my normal daily routine."

"Mine neither, I'm glad to say. When we get to the station there will hopefully be nobody about, and we might be able to wash a bit. When a train comes we'll get on it; anywhere must be better than here at the moment."

The lights of the rescue party had reached the edge of the ruined refinery. They had stopped to look at the devastation and perhaps try and work out what had happened. The initial explosion when the missile detonated inside the tower, although loud to the people beside it, may not have been heard across the runway in the terminal building.

With the prospect of people coming towards them and their questions in languages neither of them understood, Judith and Zozo pulled themselves wearily upright. Carefully placing their feet, they started to climb through the devastation, heading parallel with the airport and away from the approaching people.

seventeen

Ian had been waiting for much longer than he had expected, and was now certain that something had happened to Minda. Even allowing for sitting in the dark listening to his own heart thumping it had been a long time. In the distance he could hear someone moving, and he decided it was time for action. He had a plan; all he had to do was make it work.

His eyes now completely accustomed to the dark, Ian moved to the trolley and cleared all the cups off it, carefully putting them down on the carpet so as not to make a noise. He gathered up the spray of white-board cleaner and the plastic dust cover from the projector, and put them on the trolley.

After a moment's hesitation Ian placed his work deck on one of the chairs, and pushed it under the table out of sight. The computer contained data he absolutely needed to stop Global Asset Control's system, but it might get damaged if he took it with him. And it might get damaged or stolen if he left it. Rarely separated from his deck, this dilemma made Ian even more nervous. After some more hesitation, he moved the computer to a different chair, this time at the other side of the table, and went back to his preparations.

While Ian was listening at the door into the service corridor, his ear pressed against the wood, he heard a door being banged open. It did not sound like friendly people coming to his rescue. It was still in the distance, but moving closer, and any minute now they would see the faint trail of hot spots on the carpet that marked his footprints. Ian decided it was still sufficiently far away for him to be able to move around in the curved corridor without being seen.

Pushing the trolley ahead of him he walked quickly past the next meeting room and on to the next one. There he opened the door and, still pushing the trolley, walked in keeping the door open. This meeting room looked exactly like the other one, so Ian moved to where he had been hiding in the other one, making sure the trolley was near him and near the wall.

Once in position, Ian carefully lifted himself onto the trolley and, feet off the ground, pulled himself along the wall, and back out into the corridor. Closing the doors was difficult, especially since he did not want to make any noise.

Still lying on the trolley, Ian needed to pull himself along the wall, back the way he came. Ian soon discovered that his plan was not as easy to execute as he had thought, as there was virtually nothing to grip on. His idea was simple: the followers were watching the heat patterns left by his footprints on the floor, so they would follow him into the other room. Since the trolley wheels were at the same temperature, even with night sights they could not see the tracks leading back to the previous room.

While Ian was still in reach of the doorframe it was easy, and even then he could push with his feet. But there was the risk of moving away from the wall, so he could not push hard. Eventually he found himself stranded half way between the meeting room doors. A low-profile light switch had allowed him some more advance, but not enough. Desperately Ian tried pulling himself with his fingertips in dents on the wall where trolleys had been banged or stacked chairs dumped.

After a frustrating minute during which he did not advance at all, Ian lay back on the trolley top with his eyes shut in defeat, wondering what he could do next. Would he have to get off and push, and his plan fail? In the distance another door banged, much closer.

Suddenly Ian opened his eyes and looked up. In a second he was on his feet, and discovered he could reach the roof. The hung tiles moved up gently, allowing him to pull himself along on the metal frame. Quickly now he arrived at the previous meeting room, the one had not entered, and pushed the doors open. He was not so worried about making noise now as his attacker would be misled into going to the next, empty room.

Inside the room Ian leapt off the trolley, and pegged the doors open. He aligned the trolley with the door, and tried bracing himself behind it. For more force he put a chair on its back against a chair leg, and he could use that as an improvised starting block.

Never having been involved in fights of any kind, Ian was breathing heavily and an unaccustomed sweat had broken out. He was going to reach out and pick up the plastic dust cover, but hand in the air, he stopped. A wave of nerves swept over him. He could never achieve what he was hoping to do, an unfit, overweight desk worker could not hope to out smart and over power a professional killer. It was absurd.

Outside he could hear movement, and started to think. Ian thought quickly and had a vivid imagination. He thought of himself, and being dead. He did not like the idea, not at all, but then none of his friends would either. Then he remembered the old cliché from so many books and films: think about something to make you mad with anger, and you'd attack a bear. Instantly Zozo came to mind. He knew she would not want him dead. To his surprise Ian felt himself tense up in anger, it worked. The image of Zozo learning he was dead was enough to rebuild his determination. And if Zozo was already dead in Tchenchia, it did not matter if he died too.

Remembering what Minda had said about splat guns, Ian buttoned up his coat, and pulled the dust cover over his head. He could just about see, and the improvised hood was thick enough to stop liquids coming through. Bracing himself against the chair, he prepared to hurl the trolley out into the corridor.

———————————

After what seemed like hours of trudging through brown and black soil, Zozo and Judith arrived at last at the railway. A single, poorly-maintained track ran off into the night on one side, and into the town on the other. The exhausted girls sat down on the sleepers to rest. Zozo carefully put her head on one rail.

"What are you doing?" asked Judith.

"Listening to see if I can hear any trains," Zozo replied. "They always did in the antique westerns. Did you never do media studies?"

"No, too frivolous my father said."

"Yes, but great fun. In any case I can't hear anything on the rail, but that may mean nothing."

After a few minutes of sitting, silent, shoulder-to-shoulder, they got up and trudged towards the lights of the town. Each not wishing to discourage the other they avoided voicing the questions: was the station on this side of town, and would it be safe?

———————

Shiguru was frustrated. He had learnt that his contacts in Vienna had found Ian an escort, and that they had made contact. But now he had lost them. Ian's deck had stopped responding again, and the number for his escort was unattainable. Even the airport Marriott Flagship, where Ian had been checked in, was not answering the phone. Something was dramatically wrong, yet there was nothing he could do except wait. He was not used to this, normally he created the plans and saw they were followed, but this was not his adventure. He felt strange on the outside, yet he knew how important it was that he was patient until it was his turn.

The network trap on Judith's phone had not been triggered, and Ashley had still not listened to her messages. The only good news for Shiguru was that there were no intruders in or around the WIN building. Secreted around the building were enough surveillance cameras for him to see every part of it, not just the entrances. On his wall Shiguru now had the images from these cameras, and finally a list of who was logged in to the building. He settled back into his chair and waited.

———————

Fortunately for Judith and Zozo, the railway did not cut Androlovski in half, but skirted round the outside past the corn syrup plant. They saw shiny new rails branching off from where they were walking, heading in that direction. Stepping around the mass of points was even more tiring than the thick earth, but increasing habitation had forced them almost onto the track. If a train came they would have to leap back into someone's vegetable patch to avoid being crushed. But, as Zozo explained, trains could not run fast over that mesh of junctions.

Finally they could see the lights on the station's single platform, a good sign as another train must be due that night. Here the gardens and houses had fallen back and the track was surrounded by the rough ground that surrounds stations the world over. They passed strange discarded pieces of equipment, piles of rubbish and rubble, oil barrels, stacks of rails, sleepers and cables.

As they passed each building Zozo tried the doors. They were all either locked or gave access to small, empty rooms with a disused air at best. Some of them smelt putrid, and they quickly retreated outside. At last one of the doors gave way to a dark room that felt used, with a comfortable smell of sweat and leather.

The exhausted Judith stumbled in and leant against the wall until Zozo closed the door and found the light switch. They found themselves in a locker room, surrounded by track worker's overalls. And a mirror. Zozo could not help laughing when she saw herself, and gently pulled Judith into view, pointing at their image.

Judith smiled and slumped back down onto a bench, and shut her eyes. Zozo kept going and started looking through the lockers and cupboards. Unfortunately she soon found that the only clothes in the locker room were hi-vis safety jackets, which were even worse than their current filthy clothes as a disguise. Even the few pairs of heavy boots were far too large for either of them.

At the back of the building there was, however, a pair of sinks stamped out of stainless-steel sheets, with what looked promisingly like hot and cold taps. A liquid soap dispenser wept green tears onto the sink below. At one end there were even some rather dubious-looking towels, but in comparison to her they were quite clean. Zozo carefully found the cleanest and put it to one side.

As she waited for the water to turn hot she peeled off her outer layer of clothes. Zozo was still wearing her Bidonsol outfit, so she still wore leather jacket and jeans. The jacket shed a pile of black dust and metal shards onto the floor around it. Her boots were so clogged with soil and dust it was hard to find the ends of the laces, but they came undone eventually. Her jeans sent a cloud of dust over the floor as they collapsed to the floor.

Zozo's already dark skin had black bands round her ankles and waist where the clothes joined up. Looking at her hair she decided not to remove the T-shirt as that would get it dirtier. A cool draft blew through from a vent high up on the wall, and she was glad that it was not winter.

At last the water was running hot enough, and she simply put her head under the tap, letting the flow remove the dust and particles clogging her hair. After several soapy rinses the water did not seem quite so black and she moved on to her face and body. Even so, drying her hair turned one dirty towel filthy; Judith's longer, curly hair would take an age.

Cleaned up, Zozo felt much better. Casting her aches and pains as far back in her mind as possible, she set about soaking the cleanest towel in warm water. She carried it through to where Judith lay asleep and started to wash her face. Judith opened her eyes slowly, smiled at Zozo, raised one hand and touched her cheek, and fell asleep again. Where her hand had moved on Zozo's skin was a black dusty mark.

In the dark, still air of the meeting room Ian heard his own breath and heart beat. Then he heard something else, which his imagination took to be the creak of a cowboy boot. Dimly through his improvised visor he could see a figure pass before the door. As Ian had hoped the figure was wearing a night sight and was concentrating on following the fading heat of the footprint trail. With a deep breath Ian summoned what strength he had left, he thrust the trolley out and towards the killer.

With a turn of speed that would have surprised his gym teachers, Ian crashed the trolley hard into the side of the figure. The hand rail, positioned at kidney height, caught the other person off balance, and he fell sideways. Ian pushed as hard as he could, using his body weight for momentum.

The night sight hid any expression of surprise on his pursuer, and even when falling the professional killer raised a gun and fired at Ian's head. Ian had not expected this, and when there was a hard blow to his forehead and his vision turned red he thought he had been hit by a bullet. In the panic of an instant he did not remember the splat gun or why he was wearing the plastic hood.

With his vision turning red and his head throbbing from the impact of the pellet, Ian assumed he was mortally wounded. Enraged and convinced he was going to die, he was emboldened.

Instead of running away he grabbed the spray of whiteboard cleaner and advanced on the killer. The thug had now landed on the ground, and if not surprised before, he certainly was now. Red splat gun pellets killed instantly and without mess; for someone to continue their advance after taking a pellet straight in the face was unheard off.

Behind the pain, confusion and anger flooding Ian's mind a puzzled voice was asking why his would-be killer was trying to wriggle away from him on the ground. Why were they not attempting to shoot him again. The real answer was surprise and terror that some drips of poison would fall from the hood onto exposed skin; just as effective as a whole pellet.

Then the killer's training clicked back into action, having realised that Ian wore a hood but had bare hands. The splat gun came started to come up, but Ian's adrenaline-heightened reactions also triggered, and he aimed a kick at the hand. Never having been any good at football the kick missed the gun, but connected painfully with the wrist and the gun skittered across the floor.

Ian lost his balance with the kick and found himself on the floor beside the thug. His attacker started to jump on to him, but remembered the highly-toxic red liquid all over Ian's hood and coat. In that instant Ian remember what was left of his plan, and realised how feeble it really was. More in hope that expectation he raised the can of white-board cleaner, and sprayed it straight into his opponent's mouth and nose.

To Ian's surprise his attacker fell back convulsed with coughing. Ian leapt to his feet, the dust cover falling at his feet, and ran as fast as he could towards the other door of the meeting room. Slamming into the safety catches the door banged open and he crashed out into the public area of the hotel to find himself dazzled by bright lights. There were a couple of shouts in German, and he felt himself lifted off the ground, his coat torn off and himself thrown over a shoulder the way most people throw a towel.

eighteen

Zozo did her best to clean Judith's face, hands and feet as she slept. Fortunately her taste in shoes ran in flat-heeled brogues that had coped well with the treatment they had received. After rummaging around in the track workers' lockers Zozo had found a hair brush, which she washed several times before using to put her own hair back into its usual shape. Next she attempted to brush some of the debris from Judith's hair. After twice nearly breaking through the heavy curtain of exhaustion Zozo abandoned her efforts and let Judith sleep.

Not wanting to risk missing the last train of the night Zozo could not sleep herself. After beating her jeans and jacket against the toilet wall until all the loose particles had been dislodged she redressed. Every few minutes she looked out of the cabin towards the station.

In between checking the track, she busied herself cleaning the splat gun that she had kept hidden under her jacket. Zozo had never handled one before and was concerned that it had been damaged during the collapse of the refinery. After some shaking no more dust came out of the barrel, and Zozo risked turning the gun on. The self-test passed correctly and the status display registered "Ready." Zozo put the gun into an inner pocket of her jacket.

Eventually she noted that people were beginning to accumulate on the platform. Some were clearly there to meet friends on the train, but others had reassuringly large stacks of luggage. The next train must be going somewhere useful.

They did not know what had become of the two Global Asset Control thugs that Judith had knocked out on the tarmac, and they might be waiting for them on the platform. Or indeed other people from the base might have been flown in, including Rouge herself, although that seemed unlikely since there were only computer people and domestic staff. From her distance it was impossible to identify anyone with certainty, so she returned to Judith.

Since the train might arrive at any time Zozo started to rouse Judith, which was not easy. The towel, this time with cold water, helped, as did a glass of water. That too had had to be washed thoroughly before use. Judith slowly revived enough to understand that a train was due. That galvanised her, and she stumped through to the washroom to splash more water on herself and use the toilet. After all, neither of them knew when they next might have the chance.

Zozo now kept watch from the door all the time, keeping it shut for the light. Eventually she heard a rumble approaching them heading towards the station. She called to Judith to get ready. Neither of them had ever seen a train so large, heavy and dirty. As it ground on towards the platform they waited until the tail engine had passed, crossed the track and ran behind it. Running proved hazardous, with the sleepers, points, signals, control cables and rubbish that litters all stations, but the train had now slowed to walking pace and, with a huge release of air from its brakes, stopped.

As they had hoped the train was at least sixty years old and had manual doors on both sides of the carriages. Instead of climbing into the train at the first door, Zozo continued along the side looking for something.

"This is really old stock," Zozo noted as looked up at the doors. "These coaches don't have any safety interlocks or anything. They probably date from the Soviet era. And as for the power cars..."

"Power cars?"

"The engines. They are diesel electrics, probably bought from somewhere in Western Europe decades ago. There are four, one at the front, two in the middle, and one at the end. We must be going to climb some big gradients through serious wilderness."

"Tell me Zozo, is there anything you don't know about?" enquired the dazed Judith who had not followed Zozo's explanation at all.

"Yes, cooking for one. Politics another. Ah, here we are. Keep your fingers crossed."

She had stopped beside a carriage that looked in better condition than the others and was probably a dark blue under the long-distance dirt. Barely visible were the letters TEN picked out in white.

"Well, I can cook and politic, but I've no idea why you have stopped here."

"This is a, uh, sleeping car I think is the word. This is a Trans Euro Nuit carriage, run by the Compagnie de Wagonlit, and not by the railway company. They run all the overnight sleepers in the Union. More like rolling hotels really. This is likely to be more of a rolling hostel from the look of it."

"But we get to sleep?"

"Maybe," Zozo grunted as she swung herself up from the track bed to pull the door open. She pulled Judith up onto the steps beside her, and with a shove propelled her unceremoniously into the carriage. "Let's find the controller, buy a ticket for a twin berth and get ready for the next attack."

"Do you think they are on the train?"

"I don't know, but we should get ready anyway. And besides, we can ask the controller where the train is going."

The Trans Euro Nuit attendant had been sitting in her small cabin, with the corridor lights in her small empire already dimmed. No one in Androlovski booked sleepers; if they had enough money for a cabin they could afford to fly. She appeared as soon as Zozo opened the door, and looked in horror at the two grimy, fatigue ridden figures half collapsed on her carpet. Before she could say anything Judith pulled herself upright and spoke in her best Boston accented English.

"We nearly missed the train, and I hope you have our berth ready. My name is Judith Planter-Smail."

Even if the attendant had not spoken English, the commanding tone of Judith's voice would have made her jump.

"I'm sorry, but there is no record of the booking," she ventured in good English. She had a dream of working on some of TEN's more glamorous routes within the European Union. "But don't worry, as I've several spare berths right through to Moscow."

Judith and Zozo smiled at each other when they heard the destination.

"We'll take the best of the available twin berths," Judith commanded, pulling her credit block from the interior of her shattered Dior jacket. "Can you arrange with the controller for tickets for us through to Moscow please."

Zozo had to lower her head to hide her smirk. No one in a service role could avoid obeying Judith when she spoke like that. It must come from growing up with power and money, Zozo concluded, as she would never be able to order people about like that.

"Certainly, Ms Plonter-Snail," said the attendant. "My name is Mirov Hersten, and if I may be so bold as to indicate to you this room, where there is a shower. I will bring you towels."

"Its Miss Planter-Smail, and we will avail ourselves of the facilities in due course," Judith stated haughtily. The attendant only knew that she had said something wrong, and had not understood a word of what Judith had said.

"This is your berth, Mrs Plonter-Snail, and...?"

"Irene Dubois," Zozo said, making life easier and safer with one lie.

"Thank you Miss Hersten," Judith said, closing and locking the door.

Zozo had expected Judith to laugh after this little circus, but no, this seemed to be how she behaved in public. "Why did you tell her your real name?" Zozo asked eventually.

"I had to, it's on the credit block," Judith explained simply, and started to remove her clothes, sending clouds of dust over the clean bedspreads.

———————

Ian was sitting in a mobile incident control room parked outside the hotel at Vienna airport. He had had a shower and was drinking coffee from a Styrofoam beaker and eating a donut. On the wall in front of him was a projected image of Shiguru.

"I can't trace Judith or Ashley, or the French person..."

"Zozo," Ian interjected.

"...which is very unusual. They are all comms addicts and never switch off their phones. I've put a monitor on the news flow for anything from Tchenchia, but the only thing I've seen so far is the report of the collapse of some old chemical works."

"Shit, I think Judith, Zozo and Uri were going to hide there from the Global Asset Control people."

"It says here that four men were found dead in the remains, all of them armed in some way."

"Are you sure it said 'men'?"

"Yes, but there is no mention of casualties. They may be in hospital, or escaped, who knows."

"You know that Zozo and I are..." Ian struggled for words and felt his face colouring.

"'romantically involved'? Yes, my sources told me that." Shiguru replied. "I also know that your new friend is extremely resourceful. I'm sure she is alive."

"I hope so. But I suppose we should be doing something to fix the network. How can we get the fibre disconnected?"

"I have a problem here, Ian," Shiguru admitted. "I had hoped to get Ashley to do that for me."

"But can't you get someone from her group to do it?"

"Ashley is not the problem, it is a political issue. If I ask someone from Permanent Network to disconnect this cable it will be entered into the fault log. The fact that our security was breached will become instant news, inside and outside of WIN. We will lose our customers. Shareholder value in WIN will collapse."

"But if we don't disconnect it then Global Asset Control will be able to distort the news, so WIN will be finished too!" Ian protested.

"That is not true. Perhaps there will be, as the military say, some collateral damage, but no one will know about it. From what you have told me of them, Global Asset Control will neither destroy the world's financial stability nor advertise its success. WIN remains intact, at least long enough for you to get to London or for Ashley to show up."

"Can't you go down and do it yourself?"

"There are two problems. One is that I would not know what to do on the switches, you know as well as I do that there are a great number of them, all alike. The other problem is that my movements are carefully audited, and, I suspect, watched in other ways. If I head down to the Bowels, it will be logged, and the news will break."

"But you are in charge of security!"

"That is so, and it is my opinion that the most secure approach is to get you or Ashley to disconnect the fibre tomorrow morning. WIN will not perish if Global Asset Control completes one more job tonight."

"I suppose that I'll have to live with that, but I'm going to try and find Ashley. Do you know if her deck is still on the net?"

"Yes, but she is not answering calls."

"No problem, I think I can find her," Ian said. "Goodnight, see you in the morning."

———————

Judith was trying to brush her hair with the brush that Zozo had found. She was standing in her underwear, surrounded by a pile of black dust. "Do you suppose we could get the attendant to move us to a cleaner berth, this one seems a trifle dirty."

"But we made the mess!"

"Oh, we can give her a big tip," the wealthy Judith replied.

There was a knock at the door. Zozo leapt in one lithe curve onto the high bunk, and indicated to Judith to do the same.

"It is the attendant, Mirov Hersten," said the voice from outside. "I've put some tea in the berth next door, I thought this one might be too dirty."

"It might be a trap," hissed Zozo, pulling the splat gun from her pocket and arming it. "Tell her you're not dressed and that we'll move in a few minutes."

Judith did so, and fished her clothes up from below, wriggling into them on her bunk. "How do we tell it is not a trap?"

"My only idea is that we wait for a long time, and then move. I don't think the heavies will wait, they are more likely to break down the door first."

"I can't hear anything outside, other than the noise of the train."

"Good."

"You were going to tell me how you knew so much about weapons."

"Oh, nothing complicated. My parents worked for Dassaut Milsys, who make high-tech weapons. It is hard to be a techy and not work for the military in some way. They talked about them at home, especially the more esoteric computer based systems that my father was supposed to design."

"But the splat gun, it's not electronic is it?"

"Judith, everything made this century is electronic. This weapon has a plastic body, a ceramic barrel lining, and a set of electronics that control the launch and range of the pellets. It's is a total loss system, meaning that the poison pellets are driven by a small pellet of explosive, not a metal container like most hand guns. That means the gun and the ammunition are lighter and can fire faster."

"Who invents these things?"

"Major corporations working for governments, usually. They dream up requirements for stopping enemies, perceived and real, from being enemies. Maybe kill them, maybe maim them, incapacitate them, always stop them. Sometimes better that they are injured and then their comrades have to help them and not fight. Nice people governments. You should know. The splat gun came from a need at the beginning of the last century to eliminate hijackers from aircraft. Conventional weapons blow holes in the side of the plane, which tends to make them crash. A splat gun just wipes out one person, or maybe the people round them, but not everyone."

"Nothing has happened outside, does that mean we are safe?"

"Sadly no, but we could move rooms."

"Can we tell that there is no one on the train? Could we have taken the talk-back set from... oh." Judith stopped, her face turning grey at the realisation that Uri was dead.

"The talk-back would have been no use to us as they were speaking Russian. All we would have known was that they were on the train. That does not help much."

"Did you know that Uri was a member of the Moscow Contemporary Music Society? But you're right, Zozo, you're right. I think I was falling in love with him, and now he is gone, so suddenly. It's all so strange. I won't be able to go back to Marty..."

Zozo climbed over to the other bunk, and held Judith tight to as the tears fell. It was a long time before Judith calmed down, but Zozo was happy with that. She figured that there were Global Asset Control people on the train, but that they were on the wrong half. The two power cars in the middle of the train might climb the Urals, but stopped passengers from moving all the way from the front to the back. Their enemies would have to wait until the train stopped at a station before they could move to the other part of the train, and that would not be for several hours. Plenty of time for rest, tea, and showers.

nineteen

Minda was right, the hotel was luxurious, but Ian did not have much chance to appreciate its comforts. Even now he could not rest, even with Minda in the room, sitting impassively watching the door, and two more guards in the corridor. He had inveigled Minda into finding him a power supply for his work deck so that he could plug it into the wall. And he was using it to trace Ashley.

When they had worked together Ashley, Marc and Ian had always allowed each other full access to their work computers. He didn't suppose things had changed; he certainly had not blocked access to his friends on his deck. Even though they all replaced their machines regularly with new, faster ones, the configuration stayed the same.

From the cellular connection in the hotel, onto the Internet to London, and again via cell, Ian was able to connect to Ashley's machine. To his relief he was able to log on, but his password had expired and he was asked for a new one. That done Ian set to look around in Ashley's personal space. He knew how she arranged things, and quickly found her contact numbers. Scanning down it quickly he found two entries for a name he did not recognise: Hugo. One entry was labelled 'L', the other 'Country'.

Hugo had to be the name of the person Ashley had referred to as her scum. For some reason, in all the time Ian had known her she had never written down the family name of her men friends. Looking at the time, he realised that it was very late in Italy and very early in Tchenchia. There was no way that Global Asset Control could launch a sensible news item about Italian fertilisers at that time of day. He relaxed a bit and decided that he did not need to call her immediately.

Seeing that he had stopped typing, his bodyguard looked at him.

"Why don't you have a long, hot shower and get some sleep for what is left of the night," Minda said. She was curiously unobtrusive, having developed the art of not making her presence felt.

Ian took her advice, and still slightly damp from the shower, fell asleep more or less instantly.

"Tell me again, how does this train work?" Judith asked, over tea in the new, clean berth. Zozo and she had both had good hot showers, and filthied several of the thin towels that the attendant had produced for them. There had been soap and shampoo as well, and both women felt much better.

"The engines burn diesel, an oil-derived fuel, and those motors drive electric generators. The electricity drives electric motors which power the train."

"Why not make the diesel motors drive the wheels directly?"

"That I don't know. But I do know that there is no way through the engines in the middle of the train. Mirov says that the next stop is in three hours time. I explained that there might be people looking for us, and she worked out the rest herself. She will wake us shortly before we arrive at the stop.

"You expect us to sleep knowing that someone will be coming to kill us in a few hours?"

"Yes, because short of climbing on the roof of the train like in the old movies, they can't get at us."

It seemed as if hardly any time at all had passed when Minda woke him, saying it was time to go. She had taken off her glasses, but looked otherwise the same. Not a trace of tiredness, despite having been awake all night. During the night someone had delivered new underwear, a new top, plane tickets and a pair of dark glasses for him. Minda explained that the glasses were light-pulse safe, and that he should wear them all the time in case Global Asset Control made another attempt. The top turned out to have a hood that could cover his whole head, protecting him from pellets.

Ian pulled himself reluctantly out of bed and put on the new clothes. Someone had been well informed about his taste as they were perfect. Since he was still wearing the old 501s there was a pair of bright, patterned socks. The underpants were exactly as he liked

146

them, and the top was great. It was completely black except for a minute image of the famous Big Wheel sewn into it with some strange thread that changed colour slowly giving an impression of rotation.

He put on the heavy-looking glasses and discovered that they were not only lighter than he expected, but did not make the outside world seem dark. Minda laughed at his surprised expression and explained that they had active lenses, capable of both attenuating and amplifying light levels.

"So I can see in the dark with them?" asked Ian.

"Not quite," Minda answered, "but if there is some light available you will be able to see more clearly. I'm amazed your Zozo does not have them."

"I've only seen a small part of her impressive set of tools," Ian said, turning pink when he realised what he had said. "She may well have them. If she is still alive," he added gloomily. "Do we get breakfast?"

"On the plane," Minda said. "Let's go. You're checked out of the hotel, all that is left is to leave the building, and for the waiting limo to take us to the terminal, check in for the flight, and we're ready. We've even reserved a VIP lounge so that we can't be got at. All you have to do is try and look cool in those glasses."

"Not quite, first I have to phone Ashley."

He tried first the London number, and was directed to voice mail for Hugo Blunt. The name sounded familiar, but he could not place it. Then he tried the country number, and eventually Ashley answered, wrapped in a too-large towelling dressing gown.

"Ian!" she yelled at him down the phone. "Shit man, this is the middle of the night on a private number. What are you doing, how did you did you find me? I'm trying to sort out my life for once, and you're calling me. Shit, it's not even dawn yet."

"And I'm trying to save my life, and Zozo's and Judith's. Two people tried to kill me yesterday. The others may be dead."

"I've no patience for this nonsense. What is it?"

"Ashley, it's true. Shiguru has been trying to contact you all night."

She looked at him at him properly for the first time. She saw his face and believed him.

"OK, sorry. What do you want?"

He explained rapidly what she had to do to cut the fibre at the air conditioner where it came into the building. Only Ian had security clearance down into the bowels to finally remove the fibre, but cutting it would be just as effective.

"OK, I'll do it, but I'm out in Oxfordshire at my friend's country house. It may take me some time to get into the office."

"Well, I'm in Vienna, so you'll probably get there first."

Mirov did as she had promised, tapping on Zozo and Judith's door a few minutes before the train ground to a halt in some isolated city on the Russian steppe. Outside was still dark, with the slightest hint of dawn. Zozo tried to watch round the side of the blind, but decided that was too risky, so she settled for preparing to deal with the Global Asset Control killers.

Leaving Judith to sleep for as long as possible, Zozo removed the covers from her bunk. She hung the two blankets from the luggage rack above the door, leaving a small space between the wall and the improvised curtain. Next she pulled out her mattress and placed it over the luggage rack. Next she removed the security tag from the cover on the communications cord, and hoped that the old mechanism was connected. For want of anything better she tied a sheet round the cord and pulled the end over to where Judith lay.

This done, she woke her companion, and helped her pull the mattress up to form a barrier to hide behind, holding the sheet in a grasp tight with nerves. All they had to do now was wait.

The plane from Vienna landed at London Heathrow's Terminal Five. Ian and Minda hit the jetway running towards the Tube. It would be the fastest, safest way into the city centre. There were the usual morning crowds, so they dodged in and out of the slow-moving mass of people. Since they were coming in from the European Union there was no need to go through passport control, but they did pass the exit from the immigration hall.

Ian stopped so suddenly that Minda slammed into him from behind.

"Look!" Ian cried, pointing through the glass into one of the queues for those not holding European Union passports. He was pointing at someone with long red hair on one side of her head, but not the other.

"Who is that?" Minda asked.

"It's Rouge, the hacker from Global Asset Control," Ian said. "She set up all the networking software that we're trying to remove. She's coming to restore the program I modified so that they can complete their first contract! We've got to hurry in case Ashley has not got there."

He and Minda ran on into the morning rush hour towards the Tube.

The train was long, and it took some time before Judith and Zozo heard raised voices in the corridor: two men's voices, and the attendant. Zozo hoped she would not try anything to protect them. She had indicated that they were expecting trouble, and had explicitly told Mirov to bring any thugs to their berth so that she and other passengers would not get hurt. The only thing that Zozo had asked was that Mirov raise her voice a bit so that they could prepare themselves.

The thugs knocked on the door and one of them said "Open the door and you will not get hurt."

"Mon cul," Zozo said to herself, and she looked at Judith. Neither of them said anything.

One of the thugs kicked the door open, and it snagged in the blankets that Zozo had hung there. As he reached forward to pull them away Zozo fired the splat gun, set to spray and loaded with stun pellets, down the gap between the blankets and the wall. She scored a direct hit and the thug's body collapsed to the floor.

In the corridor they heard what sounded like muffled swearing, followed by a rustling noise.

"He's putting on hood and gloves," Zozo whispered, "so that I can't splat him. Do you feel up to using your martial arts?"

"Yes," Judith replied, "if he's off balance." She handed the end of the sheet to Zozo, and moved into a position where she could swing at the attacker.

The second thug suddenly started a charge into their berth, and Zozo pulled the sheet. The communication cord pulled out, but the train did not stop. Judith gasped as the tough fell though the blanket towards her. The plan had been that the sudden stop of the train would throw him off balance, and Judith could deliver a stunning blow. Now she was directly in his line of fire.

Except that something was wrong. Instead of firing at her, the body of the thug fell forward, one arm catching at her. Judith opened her mouth to let out an involuntary scream but nothing came out. She and Zozo were staring at the knife in his back, and the blood welling out of the wound.

Mirov stood in the corridor. "He was a Serbian," she said quietly. "My family came from Sarajevo. We have long memories."

The Tube in from Heathrow seemed to take forever, and they no longer knew if Rouge was behind or ahead of them. The ride into town seemed infuriatingly slow, but it was still quicker than taking a buggy.

As they arrived at street level Minda indicated to Ian to stay back for moment while she scanned the pedestrians milling about in Portland Village. She reappeared beside him without apparently moving, put her arm round his shoulders and pulled him into a running crouch for the remaining few hundred metres on into the WIN lobby.

Without saying anything Minda gave Ian a quick kiss on the cheek, turned and stood in the doorway, making sure that no undesirables came in after them. Despite not having slept, the travel and running she did not seem in the least tired.

Ian ignored the receptionist this time and ran to the security door. Just as the receptionist was starting to protest, the security system verified Ian's identity and let him in. Ian had forgotten that he was still wearing the old leather jacket and worn jeans; that must have shocked the receptionist even more than usual.

As soon as he was through he hit the elevator down towards level five and Ashley's office. She was not there, so he grabbed her work deck and checked to see where she was. The active badge system tracked the movements of everyone in the building, and said that Ashley was in the environment control room.

Before leaving Ashley's office Ian checked on who else was on the floor. He noticed someone called Hugo Blunt was leaving the elevator. The name matched the one he had called to contact Ashley. He pulled up the man's description and saw that he was editorial director with responsibility for crime-related news. And then he remembered: this was the person who had authorized Rouge and the cleaner who had triggered the fault in the air-conditioner. This was the person who was working for Global Asset Control.

Ian's instincts took over: he had to help Ashley. He passed the elevators and hit the fire escape down the two floors. No doubt alarms were ringing in Shiguru's security control centre, but that was good. He slammed through the door onto level seven, and saw that the door to the huge environmental control room was open. He let the door from the stairs close slowly and quietly, before moving equally quietly to the entrance.

"You listened to me on the phone this morning, at breakfast. You guessed what I was going to do. So you followed me in, and now you've betrayed not just WIN and our customers, but me!" he heard Ashley say.

"I had to, Ashley," said a voice that Ian presumed belonged to Hugo Blunt, "they were threatening me."

"How can they threaten you? What did they say?" Ashley replied, her voice high and nervous. "They could not have blackmailed you because of us?"

Ian looked round the door to see someone dressed in the multi-layered fashion of the corporate goodboy. However this goodboy was nervously holding something to Ashley's throat. Ian just made out the dull fawn of a ceramic knife. The entrance to WIN contained a well-hidden metal detector.

"No, it wasn't us," Blunt replied. "What harm had we done, except to each other? It was worse than that. They promised me power, that once the network sleeper was in place I'd be able to write my own scoops. They'd run items about other criminal networks, anything in fact, anything that I could claim to have uncovered. I'd be the most famous crime editor of all time. But of course it was all illusion. Once the sleeper was in place they had me in their power. So no scoops, and I had to do what they said."

Ian listened entranced. So this was the lover that Ashley never named. He noticed a power cable lying spare beside a spare flow meter. He moved silently into the room, and took the cable, wrapping one end round each hand.

"No, Hugo, you didn't", Ashley said. "Nobody *has* to do anything!" And with that shout she tried to turn, but the ceramic blade cut into her neck, and she started to bleed heavily. Someone screamed, but Ian did not know whether it was Ashley or Blunt; maybe it was both.

Ian took his chance, he ran behind Blunt, who was now bending over Ashley's collapsed body, and threw his improvised garrotte over his head. Ian found himself putting his knee in Blunt's back and pulling hard on the cable.

Blunt grunted and dropped the ceramic knife as he snapped upright, fighting for breath. Ian heard heavy, running feet behind him, but instead of grabbing Blunt, two pairs of strong hands grabbed his arms and pulled him away.

"This thug has broken in and seriously injured the Director of Networks here, and when I came to her aid he attacked me." Blunt croaked as he rubbed his throat. Ian realised that his clothes made the story only too convincing.

"It's not true," Ian yelled. "This man had a ceramic knife..." but he got no further as one of the security men put his hand over his mouth. Removed of the ability to speak or move, he looked down and in his horror saw that Ashley was losing blood heavily, her face already white.

Another person came running into the room, Shiguru this time. Without looking round he ran straight to Ashley, pulled something out of his pocket and placed it over the lacerations on her neck. It was a sealing bandage to promote clotting and reduce blood loss.

"Take this man away," Blunt said with an air of great authority. "While we take Ms Plank to the medical centre."

As Shiguru's men started to turn for the door with Ian, he began to wonder if Shiguru had lied, that he had set them up all along the way. He saw Shiguru open up the small leather pouch on his belt and pull out his message terminal. He ran his fingers over some icons. He checked Ashley and saw that the blood flow from her wound was too fast, that the bandage was not sealing the wound.

Ian struggled ineffectually as he was dragged to the door, and saw that Blunt was picking up the ceramic blade from where he had dropped it. The last thing Ian managed to see before he was out in the corridor was Blunt looming up over Shiguru's crouched figure, knife in hand. Now Ian knew again for sure that Shiguru was on his side.

"Come on, don't struggle so much, you'll just get tired," said one of his captors. And then they heard the scream. Perfectly trained by Shiguru, one of the men took both of Ian's arms and kept walking towards the elevator, while the other spun back into the environment control room.

His mouth finally free, Ian yelled, "Take me back, I was trying to save Ashley. It's Blunt, the other guy, that's attacking."

His captor, however, continued along to the corridor towards the elevator, Ian frantic with worry for Ashley and Shiguru, renewed his struggles to get free. He felt the heel of his heavy Bidonsol boot connect with just below his captor's knee. That seemed to hurt, and he pulled himself free.

Ian shot through the door back into the room, to see Hugo Blunt lying on the floor, his head bent to a strange angle. Shiguru was still working on his message terminal as if nothing had happened, and the other security guard was winding another bandage round Ashley's wounds. A monitor was clamped round her arm, sending medical diagnostics to the emergency crew that Shiguru had already ordered.

"Welcome back, Ian," Shiguru said without looking up. "Paul, Roger, this man is our hero. Judith and Zozo are alive, on their way to Moscow. They are now in phone range and called in a few minutes ago. They seem to have had some interesting adventures. Now Ian, while we look after Ashley, get down stairs and disconnect us properly from their fibre."

He had been so worried about Ashley that he had forgotten about the fibre. Knowing that Ashley was being looked after he ran off to the elevator, and hit the button for level ten. He emerged into the mezzanine, and repeated the procedures. As he entered the zone between inner and outer doors, he wondered how it would all end. He might be stuck there and never get out, Ashley might die from blood loss, and Zozo and the others might be killed without leaving their train.

These black thoughts were broken by the inner door opening, showing him the small metal stairwell descending into the switch room. He rattled down the stairs and headed for the switch, nervously he pulled open the cabinet doors, and there it was, the sixteenth cable where there should only be fifteen. He pulled it from the socket, disconnecting Global Asset Control's news feed completely.

To make sure of the job he unthreaded the fibre from the cable management, down to the level of the false floor. He pulled up the corner of a floor tile, put the end of the fibre between the tile and its neighbour, and stamped down on them. The fragile optical connector cracked and bent between the tiles. It could never be plugged back into the switch.

Ian stood back and heaved a sigh of relief. And then he remembered that Rouge had also been running for her systems. What if she had managed to restore her software and get the message through? With the attack on Ashley he had lost a lot of time, Rouge could easily have restored her original version of the software and pushed through the false news item.

Last time Ian has used his work deck to plug into the switch, but now it was lying useless five floors up in Ashley's office. He had to look around the machine room for a terminal. He knew that there was one always there, sitting on a trolley, but he had to find it first. At last he did, and he pushed it over to the switch.

With sweating fingers he plugged the cable in and checked the log. Nothing that could have been related to Italian agro-chemical companies had been queued. Then he looked at the verification queue. This is where items that had yet to be fully checked with their source were kept before being sent on to the news editors.

There was a news item about a labour dispute in the Southern Italian fertiliser distribution sector. It had cleared all but two of the authorization checks. Ian looked and saw it had come in from that sixteenth fibre. If Ian had taken a second longer to disconnect the cable Global Asset Control would have completed their first contract.

twenty

Outside the WIN building, paramedics were loading Ashley Plank into an ambulance. They had a blood recycler clamped to her neck, amongst other equipment. She was unconscious and very pale. Shiguru was at her side, and watched anxiously as the vehicle pulled away towards the hospital.

Almost immediately a police van arrived, and Shiguru welcomed the serious-faced officers into the building. There were many things to be talked about, not the least of which was the body of Hugo Blunt, still lying in the environmental control room seven floors underground.

In Moscow a huge diesel-powered train pulled into the central station, dirty from the long, hard haul across the vast expanse of Russia. It contrasted sharply with the smart electric commuter trains and the sleek rail runners connecting to St Petersburg and the European Union countries.

Two people clad in grey one-piece suits and dark glasses ran along the train until they came to the TEN carriage and leapt on board, clearly looking for someone. They met up with two people in the sleeping car, and there was some discussion. A group of police with two stretchers and a body bag walked along to the same carriage. The two people from the train also donned dark glasses and thin hoods, and were led off the train towards the Hilton International hotel next door for a shower and some food.

The carriage attendant beckoned the police on board, indicating to bring the body bag with them. They emerged later carrying the full bag and another inert body. Another TEN attendant arrived to look after the other passengers, while the original left with the police.

A figure with bright red hair, short on one side of her head and long on the other, slipped out an inconspicuous door in Tower Hill tube station. She was soon lost in the usual cosmopolitan tide of humanity that swelled through the London Underground. She was heading for the Piccadilly Line and out to Heathrow.

In Moscow, Zozo wanted to get to Paris, and then an onwards connection to Edinburgh. Judith was enquiring about flights to Boston.

Zozo was able to get a place on a rail runner leaving in two hours for Paris, via an interesting variety of places she had never visited. One of the grey-clad figures was to accompany her to make sure nothing untoward happened. She bridled at being treated like that, but realised it was for her own safety. She was a lot happier to learn that her guardian angel also had a telephone that would work on the runner.

Judith called her father to let him know that she was coming home. She did not seem surprised when she learnt that he had tried to contact her.

Before they separated, Zozo and Judith held each other tightly, and promised to meet again soon, somewhere safe.

An electronic mail message arrived in the subscriptions department of WIN cancelling a full-service news account in the name of Global Asset Control. It was greeted with some dismay as no one had ever cancelled an account before.

A senior accountant tried to reply to the mail, but found that the address from which it had been sent no longer existed. Neither did the bank account from which the account had been paid. At least they had not lost a future subscription, he thought, as he looked up the procedure for cancelling a subscription.

In Paris a high-tech office was suddenly empty of people and the signs had vanished. The owner of the office was alarmed to find that his tenant had apparently vanished, without paying any bills. The company that had seemed so real and reliable had evaporated. All traces of its existence seemed to have scrubbed away as if it had never been. But they had left a large number of expensive computers that more than made up for the debts. The strange thing was that all the storage in the machines had been completely erased, and any paper that had mentioned the name of the company had been shredded.

Far out in Tchenchia a huge shadow moved slowly across the endless miles of corn. Not far away a pilotless helicopter took off for one last run, ferrying people and their personal possessions to the nearest town. Behind them they left a large number of crates of computer equipment.

The shadow was caused by a heavy transport airship, underneath which hung an empty container, a massive bulldozer, and two empty cradles. Arriving over an abandoned missile base, it lowered the bulldozer, the container, and a crew cabin.

When the cabin reached the ground the crew started to load the crated computers into their container. When they were done, two of them took a metal case over to the two concrete disks covering what once were missile silos. From the metal case they took explosive charges, and set them on the middle of the disks. Retiring behind the nearest building they set of two small explosions. The disks cracked and huge shards of concrete fell into the deep holes, crushing the temporary floors that had been built inside the silos.

One of the men mounted the massive bulldozer and started to demolish the buildings, reducing them to rubble. It was easy work as the buildings were old and had been built of prefabricated concrete panels. All he had to do was push the walls. Soon there were just a few piles of rubble, and these were rapidly pushed into the silos, filling them up completely.

As the bulldozer was pulled back up to the airship, one empty cradle was lowered. The airship manoeuvred very slowly until the cradle was directly over the biomass power generator. The crew disconnected the heavy power cables and hooked up the cradle to the generator's suspension points. They stood back and watched as the generator was winched up into the air.

Finally the crew cabin was wound back up to the airship, and they headed off towards Androlovski to collect the drone shuttle. All that was left behind was a clear circle in the cornfields. A few concrete bases showed where once buildings had stood. Broken concrete and brick rubble filled the old silos, and the pile of corncobs marked where the generator had been.

Next season the farmers would plough the ground and plant corn, and eventually the site would disappear completely.

Ian left the bowels of WIN and headed up to the fifth level and Ashley's office. He was met there by one of Shiguru's staff, who told him about Ashley being taken to hospital, and that the police were there and would need to interview him. Ian sank, exhausted, into Ashley's chair. He nodded quietly, and asked the man to tell Shiguru that they had succeeded, and that he would wait in Ashley's office.

As the security guard left the room Ian noticed he was limping slightly, and Ian realised it was one of the men who had held him. He had never seen his face, as he had left the room too fast.

Ian had a look at his work deck, and raided some spare parts from Ashley's deck. Soon he had his system working normally again. Out of habit he started to check his e-mail, looking as usual for anything out of the ordinary. There were two messages that immediately leapt to his attention.

One from a user called rouge at a machine called scarlet, somewhere in London. He realised that scarlet was the name of the machine in the sewers. He opened the message: "Congratulations, you won. This time." It was signed Rouge. He stared at it for a while in astonishment.

The other message was from someone in a public terminal in a hotel in Moscow. At first he did not recognise the name, Nadine Berthaud. Suddenly he realised it was from Zozo. His heart pounding he looked at the text: "We have arrived in Moscow, still alive, but battered. Judith is going home. I need lots of tender loving care, I'm sure you do too. Clear me some drawer and hanging space. I'll make my own pile. I love you, Zozo."

Printed in Great Britain
by Amazon.co.uk, Ltd.,
Marston Gate.